BOUNTY HUNTING . . .
FOR GLORY

"Do you know who Clint Adams is?"

Stark sat forward in his chair so abruptly that Russell sat back in his, even though the wide expanse of his desk was separating them.

"The Gunsmith?"

"That's right. Do you think you can take him?"

"Is that the job?" Stark asked. Russell thought he detected a note of eagerness in the man's voice.

Stark knew he had agreed to this job for a lot less than Russell would have paid, but if he could kill the Gunsmith it would *make* his reputation.

Some things were more important than money. . . .

The Gunsmith *series*

J. R. Roberts

Books 127 – 189

Ghost Town
The Caliente Gold Robbery
Golden Gate Killers
The Road to Testimony
The Witness
The Great Riverboat Race
Two Guns for Justice
Outlaw Women
The Last Bounty
Valley Massacre
Nevada Guns
Deadly Gold
Vigilante Hunt
Samurai Hunt
Gambler's Blood
Wyoming Justice
Gila River Crossings
West Texas Showdown
Gillett's Rangers
Return to Deadwood
Blind Justice
Ambush Moon
Spanish Gold
Night of the Wolf
The Champion with a Gun
Lethal Ladies
Tolliver's Deputies
Orphan Train
The Magician
Dakota Guns
Seminole Vengeance
The Ransom

The Huntsville Trip
The Ten Year Hunt
The Empty Gun
The Last Great Scout
The Wild Women of Glitter Gulch
The Omaha Heat
The Denver Ripper
The Wolf Teacher
Chinaville
The French Models
Crime of Passion
The Elliott Bay Murders
Funeral for a Friend
The Hanging Women
Jersey Lily
Gunquick
Grave Hunt
Triple Cross
Buried Pleasures
Wild Bull
The Queensville Temptress
Chinatown Assassin
The Challenge
Winning Streak
The Flying Machine
Homestead Law
The Biloxi Queen
Six for the Money
Legbreakers and Heartbreakers
The Orient Express
The Posse from Elsinore

For books 1 - 126 go to:
www.speakingvolumes.us

THE GUNSMITH

#131

THE WITNESS

SPEAKING VOLUMES, LLC
NAPLES, FLORIDA
2016

THE GUNSMITH
#131 THE WITNESS

ISBN 978-1-61232-734-1

THE GUNSMITH

#131

THE WITNESS

J.R. ROBERTS

Chapter One

When Clint Adams received the message from Jim West to meet him in Garden City, Arizona, he hadn't known what to expect—from West, *or* from the city. As it turned out, it wasn't a city at all, just a small town that had very little to recommend.

Uncharacteristically, West was three days late, but Clint knew West well enough to know that with the meeting preset, he *would* finally show up, or send a representative. Meanwhile, he had been spending his time with a woman named Carol Sanger.

Carol was tall and dark-haired, slimly built but for large, round, firm breasts. It was a phenomenon Clint had found in a few women over the years; slender everywhere else but in the chest. Another thing about her was that she worked in the gunshop. He had gone there for some gun oil, and tension had filled the air between them as soon as they saw each other—*sexual* tension.

They went to bed the first night he was in town—which is where they were now, after having spent their third night together.

Carol was curled up against him and he could feel her gentle breathing on the back of his neck. Her skin was dark, and her nipples were *very* brown, and large. He tried to turn over without waking her so he could watch her sleep, but her eyes fluttered open and she caught him.

"Again?" she asked.

He smiled and said, "I was going to watch you while you slept, but now you've ruined it."

"I never knew a man who took so much pleasure in just watching a woman sleep."

"A woman as beautiful as you would be hard *not* to watch."

"I also never heard a man talk the way you do," she said, shaking her head.

He leaned over her and kissed her right nipple, sucking it. She drew her breath in and held it, closing her eyes. She had very sensitive nipples. In fact, that first night he had made her climax just by sucking her breasts. Later, while he again worked on her breasts and nipples with his mouth as she rode him, she went so wild with orgasm that the bed began to bounce.

"You'll give me a heart attack," she said now as he moved his mouth to her other breast.

She moaned when he nibbled her breasts, groaned when he kissed her soft belly, and cried out—*loudly*—when he delved into her with his tongue, his nose nestled securely in her wiry, black pubic hair.

• • •

She watched him as he dressed, her head propped up on her hand. Absently, her hand stroked her right breast, tugging lightly at the nipple. He had never seen a woman touch herself so unconsciously.

"If you don't stop doing that I'll be out of these clothes faster than I got into them."

"Doin' what?"

"Rubbing yourself that way."

She looked down at her hand, as if she were just noticing what it was doing.

"Oh," she said, removing her hand, "I'm sorry. Does it bother you?"

"It doesn't *bother* me," he said, "it *affects* me."

"Oh," she said, her hand straying to her breast again, "good."

"I've got to go, Carol," he said, clenching his teeth.

She dropped her hand and said, "To look for your friend?"

"Either him or a message from him."

"I hope you don't find neither," she said. "If you do, you'll leave me."

"It has to happen sometime, Carol."

"I know that," she said. "Don't think I don't know that. If there was a way I *could* make you stay—"

"We talked about this before—"

"I know, I know," she said, moving her hand away from her breast now. "I'm not makin' any demands on you, Clint."

"Good girl," he said. "It's better this way, believe me. This way neither one of us is going to get hurt."

"You keep on believin' that, Clint Adams," she said, "you just keep on believing that."

• • •

Clint's first stop was the hotel desk. He asked the old man if West had registered yet.

"I'll give you the same answer I been givin' you for the past three days," George Sanger, Carol's father, said. "No!"

"Thank you," Clint said, with exaggerated politeness. "I'll see you later."

Clint's next stop was the telegraph office—and wasn't that a shock to find out that Garden City had one—but there was no message waiting for him.

Damn that West, Adams was thinking as he left the telegraph office. One more day, he swore to himself, I'll give you one more day!

Sure. He knew damned well that he'd stay here as long as it took to either see West, or receive a message from him. They had that kind of friendship.

Clint had breakfast in a small cafe he had found, where the food was better than the food at the hotel. Still, it was *barely* edible.

He lingered over a second pot of coffee—which was *just* this side of drinkable—and wondered what Jim West wanted with him this time. It was always *something* very dangerous, something he didn't have time to work on himself, but trusted to no one else. West was always able to convince the United States Secret Service to use Clint Adams when those situations arose. William Masters Cartwright, the current head of the Secret Service, didn't like Clint, but always agreed. He knew that Clint got the job done.

He rose, paid his bill, and left the cafe just in time to see a rider coming down the street.

He stepped out into the street to block the rider's path, and when the man reined in his mount to keep from trampling him, Clint Adams said to Ross Martin, "Why am I not surprised to see you?"

Martin stared down at Clint and said, "Jim couldn't make it, Clint."

"He never can."

It seemed as if every time Jim West asked Clint for his help, he was never there to explain just what it was he needed help with. He was always off doing something else—which, when you thought about it, was *why* he needed Clint's help.

It probably made sense.

Ross Martin, for the past year or so, had been Jim West's partner.

"I'm sorry I'm late," Martin said. "Were you here on time?"

"I've been here . . . a short while," Clint said.

"Well, just let me get my horse taken care of and you can show me where to get a decent breakfast."

As Clint watched Martin ride away he smiled a wolfish smile and wondered if he should take Martin to the hotel to sample the food.

Chapter Two

"Jesus," Martin said, pushing his plate as far away from him as he was able to, "if that wasn't the worst breakfast I ever had it was pretty damn close."

"Really?"

Martin eyed Clint suspiciously but decided not to press the matter of the chosen place for breakfast.

"My lateness was unavoidable," Martin said, "as is Jim's absence."

"Neither surprises me."

"Jim didn't get word to me until—well, that doesn't matter," Martin said, waving away his explanations. "What matters is that I explain the assignment to you to see if you will accept it."

"And what *is* the assignment?"

"It's a bodyguarding job," Martin said.

"That's not my usual area of expertise," Clint said.

"We know that," Martin said, "but this is important, Clint."

"*How* important?"

"Have you ever heard of a man named Robert Russell?"

"Can't say that I have. What's he done to attract the attention of the government?"

"Right now the government is charging him with conspiracy to commit murder."

"Isn't that kind of hard to prove?"

"It is," Martin said, "without a witness."

"Ah," Clint said as the light dawned, "and you have a witness, don't you?"

"We do."

"And you want someone to keep this witness alive."

"I do."

"And that someone is me."

"Exactly right," Martin said. "Our witness can place Russell squarely in the middle of a conspiracy to murder a rival rancher."

"Why?"

"For refusing to sell his land."

"That's been done before," Clint said. "Ranchers have fought and killed each other over land a million times. The same question always comes up. Why didn't he just make another offer?"

"He did," Martin said, "several offers. They were all turned down."

"That's every man's right."

"Not the way Russell sees it," Martin said. "He saw that this man was in his way, and he conspired to have the man removed."

"Why would a case like this involve the government?" Clint asked.

Martin looked around to see if they were speaking in total privacy. Breakfast was over for the most part, and there was only one other table taken, and it was on the other side of the room.

"The United States government is interested in the same land."

"Why?"

Martin waved his hand and said, "That's not important. Let's just say they were planning to buy up a lot of the same land that Robert Russell has been buying—"

"Only if he got there first, it's going to cost the government a lot more money than it would have."

"Exactly."

"And if Russell is buying the same land, he must have known something in advance."

"You're doing fine."

"That means that someone in the government gave him the information," Clint said. "If you can nail Russell down on the conspiracy charge, you can work a deal with him for the name of the informant."

Martin spread his hands and said, "There, you have it!"

Clint leaned forward and said, "Russell isn't going to let this witness live—if he knows who he is."

"Right."

"The witness is a woman?"

"That's correct."

That didn't really matter to Clint. What did matter was that there was still a catch somewhere in the story.

"Where's the catch, Ross?" Clint said. "Let me have it now so I don't find out about it on my own."

"There is no catch," Martin said. "Granted, there is some ground to cover—"

"Ground to cover? How so?"

"Well, we'll be needing the witness in D.C., to testify."

"And?"

"And the witness lives in Arizona."

"You want me to keep the witness alive and transport her from Arizona to Washington, D.C.?"

"Exactly."

"And do it alone?"

"Well," Martin said, "the government really can't offer you all that much support as you take her cross-country, Clint."

"Uh-huh," Clint said. "And the government doesn't want the word to get out that they're interested in this particular piece of land, right?"

"Let's just say that the government wants to keep a low profile on this," Martin said. "Once you reach Washington, D.C., however, Cartwright will have some men there to assist you."

"Oh," Clint said, "and I can count on that, right?"

Martin knew how Clint—and West—felt about Cartwright. In fact, he shared their feelings.

"On this one I think you can," Martin said. "Cartwright wants to get this done ... which is why he agreed with Jim to turn this over to you. He knows that if anyone can get the witness to Washington alive—"

"Spare me that part, Ross," Clint said, holding up his hand. "Just tell me how do you expect me to do that? If Russell knows about her he's certainly not going to sit on his hands while I take her from Arizona to Washington."

Martin leaned forward and said, "I'm not worried, Clint. I figure you'll find a way."

Chapter Three

"All right," Clint said, after they had ordered another pot of coffee, "tell me about the witness."

"Her name is Sally Murcer," Ross Martin said.

"How did you find her?"

"She sent a telegraph message to Washington, telling us that she saw and heard Robert Russell planning to kill a man named Slim Duncan. He's the other rancher I told you about."

"And how was this Sally Murcer in such a position?" Clint asked.

"She works for Russell."

"Isn't that going to taint her testimony a bit?"

"That doesn't matter," Martin said.

"No, it doesn't," Clint said, suddenly aware of the catch, "because you don't really expect her to make it. You think she's going to be killed somewhere along the way, and I'm going to be a witness to it—and then you can pin *that* on Robert Russell and make your deal."

"That's not true . . . and even if it was, Clint, it's not *me*—"

"Ross—"

Martin held his hands up to ward off Clint's pro-testations.

"Of course there *is* a possibility that she won't make it to Washington, but Jim and Cartwright have every confidence that you and she will, Clint. Jim wouldn't set you up like that."

"No," Clint said, "but Cartwright would."

Ross didn't reply.

"And if I do manage to get her there alive?" Clint asked. "Is that going to ruin your—I'm sorry, the *government's*—plans?"

"No, we'll just go ahead with her as a witness."

"And what if I don't take this job?"

"Then she'll probably die without ever having left Arizona."

Clint frowned at Martin and knew that the man—standing in for Jim West—had gone and done it to him again, gotten him to accept an assignment he knew he shouldn't touch.

"All right, where does this gal live?"

"A town called Wells, Arizona. It's two day's ride from here."

And there was the reason for meeting in a nowhere town like Garden City.

"What happened to Duncan?"

"He's alive," Martin said, "and he'll testify against the man who actually tried to kill him."

"When do you need Sally Murcer in Washington?"

"Within the next two weeks."

"I'll need some money," Clint said.

"For what?"

"Traveling expenses."

Martin frowned.

"How do you expect to travel?"

"I'm not going to tell you that, Ross."

"Why—"

"There's a leak, remember?" Clint said. "My route will be known only to me."

Martin opened his mouth to protest, then stopped, thought a moment, and said, "That's an excellent strategy, Clint."

"Thank you. Now if you'll excuse me, I'll see to my horse."

"You'll be leaving right away?"

"It's still early enough and I don't see any reason to waste the day," Clint said. "I just have to say good-bye to someone and I'll be off. You'll be in Washington, I suppose?"

"No," Martin said, "I have another assignment myself, which is why I couldn't take this one. Cartwright will meet you in Washington."

"Oh good," Clint said, "something to look forward to. Just let him know that I'll only make contact to let him know that we are still en route," Clint said. "If he doesn't hear from me for, oh, three days then you'll know that we're not coming."

Martin stood and said, "Good luck."

"I'm going to need it, Ross."

As the two men rose to leave Martin said, "Oh, there's something else you should know."

"And what's that?"

"She may need some persuading to testify."

"I thought you said *she* got in touch with you."

"She did," Martin said, "but since then there's been an attempt on her life. She, uh, might have changed her mind by now."

When Clint entered the hotel Carol was working behind the desk.

She looked at him with a ready smile, but when she saw his face her look changed.

"Your friend is here."

"How did you know that?"

"It's all over your face," she said. "You came to say good-bye."

"I have to go, Carol."

"Wait," she said, quickly, "I'll get somebody to take over—"

Clint touched her hand, cutting her off.

"That wouldn't be a good idea, Carol," he said. "Let's just say good-bye here."

"But Clint—"

He leaned over and kissed her. When he drew back she just stared at him.

"Maybe," she said, finally, "you'll be back this way some time."

"Sure," he said. "Maybe."

He went up to his room and collected his gear. When he came down he noticed that she was no longer behind the desk. Her father looked up and scowled at him as he was coming down the stairs, and Clint left the hotel. He knew that Carol's father wouldn't care if he *never* came back this way again.

Chapter Four

During the two day ride to Wells, Arizona, Clint thought about the attempt that had already been made on the life of Sally Murcer.

"Somebody took a shot at her, is all," Martin had said, "but she might be a little nervous about it."

"I'll bet. What about the local sheriff? Is he honest?"

"The sheriff?" Martin shrugged. "As far as we can tell, yes."

"But the rest of the town is in Robert Russell's pocket, right?"

"With a man that wealthy, I guess that's a distinct possibility."

"So wouldn't it be unusual for the local lawman to be his own man?"

"Perhaps you just have a cynical outlook on local law," Martin said.

"When there's a lot of money involved it becomes easy for a lawman to look the other way."

"Not this one," Martin said. "At least, I hope not. You'll be able to tell more when you meet him."

"Will I have to?" Clint asked. "I'd like to get in and out of that town as quickly as I can, with as few people knowing about it as possible."

"Miss Murcer is in his care."

"I'd say that was a hell of a chance to take, Ross, but I realize that if she's dead when I get there it could still work in your favor."

"Not *my* favor—"

"Oh, right, right," Clint said, "the *government's* favor. What's the sheriff's name?"

"Winfield, Sheriff Ted Winfield."

"Never heard of him," Clint said.

It might have been easier if he had. At least he'd know whether he could trust the man or not.

He had also taken the two days on the trail to plan his route to Washington, D.C. It would involve a lot of horseback riding, and a couple of train rides. He hoped that the young woman would be up to the strain that she was going to be under.

If she wasn't, she might very well end up dead.

Wells, Arizona, was a larger town than Garden City, and still growing. Clint was sure that a man like Robert Russell would have had a lot to do with that. There were sure to be many townspeople who thought that Robert Russell was the father of their town. He was going to have to keep a low profile on why he was in town.

He left his horse at the livery and carried his gear to the first hotel he saw.

"Just passing through?" the clerk asked. He was in his forties, balding, and potbellied.

"That's right."

"Could be you'll decide to stay a spell," the man said. "It's a nice town."

Clint finished signing in and said to the man, "Can I have my key, please?"

"Sure can," the man said, handing him the key. He looked at the register and added, "Enjoy your stay in Wells, Mr. . . . Adams."

"Thank you."

Clint went up to the room, dropped off his gear, and then left the hotel in search of the sheriff's office. On the way he passed a saloon and decided to stop in for one drink. Once he had the woman in his custody he wouldn't be making many stops at public places like cafes, hotels, and saloons.

The saloon was small and only half full. It was late afternoon, but still too early for the saloons to start filling up. He went to the bar and ordered a beer from a tall, thin bartender with a cowlick.

"Just get into town?" the man asked, setting a beer down in front of him.

"That's right."

"Passing through?"

Clint looked at the man and said, "Yes."

"Might be you'll decide to stay," the man said.

"Because it's a friendly town?"

"That's right."

Both the desk clerk and the bartender had seem unusually interested in a stranger—even more so

than people were *usually* interested in strangers.
Clint decided to finish the beer quickly and get over
to the sheriff's office. Something definitely was not
right here.

He was halfway through the beer when two men
appeared at the bar, one on either side of him. He
looked at them and recalled that they had been seated
at a table when he entered.

"You got business in town?" one of them asked.

He looked from one to the other, then back at the
one who had spoken.

"Could be I do."

"My friend asked you a question," the second man
said.

"I heard him," Clint said, and ignored both men.

"Listen, funny man—" the man continued, putting
his hand on Clint's shoulder.

"Take your hand off me," Clint said coldly.

"Now look—" the first man said, moving closer.

Clint grabbed the first man by the thumb of the
hand that was on his shoulder and twisted. He'd
been through this before, in a lot of towns. There
were always men who thought they were tough.
The man either had to go to his knees or have his
thumb snapped. He looked at the other man and said,
"Back off."

"Easy, mister . . ." the man said, raising his hand.

"Take your gun out with your thumb and forefinger
and put it on the bar."

"Whatever you say," the man said, nervously. He
did as he was told and then put his hands back in
the air, as if Clint was holding a gun on him.

Clint was holding the thumb of the other man's gunhand, so he said to him, "Take yours out with your other hand and slide it away from you."

"Jesus, mister," the man said, "my thumb—"

"Do it," Clint said, twisting the thumb.

"Ow, all right!"

The second man put his gun on the floor and pushed it away from him.

"Bartender, you in on this?"

"Not me," the barkeep said, showing Clint both of his palms.

To the man whose thumb he was holding he said, "Come on, friend, walk me to the door."

He eased the pressure enough for the man to rise and walk to the door with him.

"When I let you go," Clint said, "go and sit in a chair."

"Sure, sure," the man said. He was sweating profusely from the pain.

Clint released his thumb and the man hurried to a chair and cradled his thumb in his lap.

"A real friendly bunch," Clint said to them, and backed out of the saloon. He kept his eye on the door as he walked away, but no one came out after him, and he continued on to find the sheriff's office.

Chapter Five

When Clint entered the sheriff's office, behind the desk was a homely man in his thirties who wore a star on his chest. Clint guessed that this was Sheriff Winfield.

"Sheriff Winfield?"

"That's right," the man said, looking Clint over.

"My name's Clint Adams," Clint said. "I'm here about Sally Murcer."

"Oh, right," Winfield said. "Adams . . . you're not—"

"Yes, I am," Clint said.

The look on the man's face changed and he stood up.

"Where would she be right now?" Clint asked.

"She's at the rooming house," Winfield said. "I got a man watching her. I'll give you directions—"

"If you've got a man on her," Clint said, "maybe you

better walk me over. It'll save us maybe shooting at each other."

"Oh, sure," Winfield said, coming around the desk. He was in his early forties, about five-ten and slender except for a potbelly. "This way."

"Thanks."

They left the office and Clint followed the lawman to the north end of town. The rooming house was a large two-story house that looked old, but like it had just been repaired.

The sheriff knocked on the door, which was answered by a woman in her sixties. Her gray hair was kept in a bun behind her head, but some strands had come loose and she was swatting at them with her hand.

"Sheriff."

"We're here to see Sally, Molly."

"Come on in, then."

Inside Winfield introduced Clint to Molly McGuane.

"You here to keep Sally safe?" Molly asked.

"That's right."

"You better do a proper job of it," Molly said, "or you'll have to answer to me."

"I'll keep that in mind, ma'am."

"They're in the sittin' room," Molly said. "Go ahead in."

"Thanks, Molly."

Clint followed Winfield into the sitting room. There were two people there, playing checkers. One of them was a young deputy in his early twenties, who looked up quickly as they entered.

"Easy, Rafe," Winfield said. "This fella's here to see Sally."

The woman had been sitting with her back to the door, and when she turned Clint stared. She had long red hair, green eyes, and clear, pale skin. Her eyes caught his and held them, and she bit her lush bottom lip as she looked him over. He licked his own lip as a result.

She was stunning.

"You're my bodyguard?" the woman asked, standing up. She was tall, almost five-eight. She had full breasts and, unlike Carol Sanger, the rest of the body to go with it: strong, wide shoulders to support the breasts, wide hips, solid legs. A big woman.

Clint looked at her and said, "If you're Miss Murcer then I'm your bodyguard, and your escort."

"Well, it's about time you got here," she said.

Clint bit back his initial response and said, "I came as soon as I was notified."

She approached him and stuck out her hand. He took it and was surprised at the strength of her grip. Not only was she a big woman, but a healthy, strong one.

"Happy to meet you, Mr. Adams," she said. "Now, when do we leave?"

"Tomorrow morning, if that's soon enough for you," Clint said.

"*Now* would be soon enough, but tomorrow will be fine," she said. She turned back to the deputy, who had been watching with no expression on his face.

"Thanks for baby-sitting, Rafe, but you'll understand if I run out on our game? And forgive me?"

"Sure, Sally," the man said. "It's no fun being cooped up anywhere."

Clint thought that the deputy probably could have stood being cooped up with Sally Murcer indefinitely. The way the man was looking at her, Clint was sure there were some strong feelings here, if only on the man's side.

"Before we leave, Miss Murcer—"

"Call me Sally."

"Sally—before we leave I'd like to talk to the sheriff about something."

"A problem?" Winfield asked.

Clint explained the reception he had received since arriving in town and finished up with the encounter at the saloon.

"Describe the two men," Sally Murcer said. Clint did and she was nodding her head, saying, "They work for Bob Russell."

"What about the hotel clerk?" he asked.

"Russell owns that saloon, but he doesn't own the hotel," Winfield said. "Still, a few dollars to the desk clerk and he'd own him right quick. The word went out that a stranger would be coming to town to escort Sally out. I guess maybe the boys were checking you out."

"What happened to them?" she asked.

"I disarmed them."

"Alone?" she asked, looking surprise. "Without killing them?"

"There really wasn't anyone around I could ask for help," Clint pointed out.

"Mr. Adams—"

"Clint."

"Clint, I get the feeling I'm in good hands," Sally Murcer said, smiling and taking Clint's breath away.

"Still," she went on, "I'm not all that sure I still want to be a witness."

"Maybe we could talk about that over something to eat, Miss Murcer."

"Sally," she said, "and I know just the place."

"I don't know that we should be seen in a public place—"

"I know a small cafe where we'll be safe," she said. "It's run by a friend of mine."

"Is the food any good?" Clint asked, remembering the meals he had eaten in Garden City.

"It's *very* good."

"Well, all right—"

"Great," she said, taking hold of his arm.

"She's your responsibility now, Adams, right?" Winfield asked.

"That's right, Sheriff."

"Still . . . check in with me before you leave tomorrow," Winfield said, looking first at Sally and then at Clint. "I want to be sure you get off all right."

"We'll do that, Sheriff," Clint said. "Lead the way, Sally."

Chapter Six

Sally Murcer led him to a small cafe on the side street. Clint was aware of the looks they were getting from the people on the street.

"Does everyone in this town know what we're doing?" he asked.

"I'm afraid I made a big mistake when I contacted Washington by telegraph to make myself available as a witness," Sally Murcer said.

When they entered the cafe, a handsome woman in her forties greeted them. She was built along the same full-bodied lines of Sally Murcer, a few inches shorter, ten years or more older, but with something of the same affect on men, he was sure. Clint noticed that the place was completely empty of customers.

"Sally, how are you?" the woman asked. The two women embraced a moment.

"I'm fine, Linda," Sally said. "This is my official protector, Mr. Clint Adams. Clint, this is Linda Contact. I'm afraid being my friend has affected her business somewhat."

"Never mind that," Linda said, eyeing Clint. "I'm pleased to meet you, Mr. Adams. Come and sit and I'll get some coffee. You two want dinner?"

"Definitely," Sally said before Clint could reply. She turned to him and said, "Linda is the best cook in town and I could really use one of her meals after the slop I ate in the sheriff's office the last few days."

"I'll let you start on the coffee and some biscuits while I cook," Linda said.

"Thanks, Linda."

Linda Contact went into the kitchen and Clint said, "Let's take that table over there."

"In the corner? Oh, I see it," Sally said. "All right, that's fine."

Clint sat with his back to the wall so he could see the entire room and the front door. Sally was going to sit across from him with her back to the door but he made her move and sit on his left.

Linda came back with a pot of coffee, two cups, a basket of biscuits, and some butter.

"That should hold you for a while," she said, and went back into the kitchen.

Sally poured coffee for the both of them and they each buttered a biscuit.

"What do you need to know?" she asked him.

"Actually, I don't need to know anything, Sally," he said. "My job is to get you to Washington safely to testify."

"Well, what happens if I get killed along the way?"

she asked. "Maybe I could just tell you what I know so you could testify—"

"I wouldn't be able to," he said. "I can't testify to something I didn't see."

"No, of course not."

"Sally, I can understand why you'd be nervous—"

"Thank you."

"—but the government really needs you on this. I'm sure you wouldn't have contacted them if you weren't willing to testify in the first place."

"I'm afraid I got carried away with myself, Clint," Sally said. "I should have thought first."

"But you didn't," Clint said. "Frankly, I don't think you'd be safe even if you decided *not* to testify now."

Sally frowned and said, "You're probably right."

"Then are we set to go to Washington?"

She eyed him with a worried look and said, "Oh, God, I guess so. What route will we be taking?"

"I'd rather not say, if you don't mind."

She stared at him for a moment, then said, "You don't think *I'd* tell anyone, do you?"

"That's not the point," he said. "I'd just rather keep that information to myself for the time being."

"You're real careful, aren't you?"

"Would you have me be less than careful?"

"Hell, no," she said, buttering another biscuit, "as far as I'm concerned, you're the boss."

It was nice to hear, but she *was* a woman, and it would be interesting to see how long that attitude lasted.

Chapter Seven

The food was as good as Sally had promised. It didn't even need to be compared to the food in Garden City, it would have been good anyway. Her friend Linda was not only the best cook in town, but one of the best Clint had ever run across, and he told her so after the meal.

"Thank you, sir," Linda said with a curtsy. It was an odd thing to see a forty-year-old woman curtsy, but she did it well. "For that you get another piece of apple pie—if you want it."

"I do," Clint said.

"Sally?"

"Not me. I'm stuffed."

"I'll get yours," Linda told Clint.

"She likes you," Sally said after Linda had gone off for the pie.

"Well . . . I'm glad. She seems very nice."

28

"She's impulsive, too."

"Which means?"

"I'm just warning you," she said, "but I don't expect you have to be warned about women."

"Thanks anyway. I was wondering what it was you did for Robert Russell?"

She blinked and sat back in her chair. "Oh," she said, studying him. "Well, believe it or not I was one of his ranch hands."

"Cowhand?"

"Ranch hand," she said, "but that included working with cows, and horses, and fence posts."

"Kind of an odd job for a woman, isn't it?"

"It's what I wanted to do," she said, "and I did it pretty well."

"I'll bet you did."

Linda came back with Clint's second piece of pie. The look on her face said that she thought she had interrupted something, so she left the pie with a smile and retreated to the kitchen.

"Can you use a gun?" Clint asked Sally.

"Yes."

"A handgun?"

"I have one in my room," she said. "I haven't been wearing it because I didn't want to look like I was looking for trouble."

"Wise move," he said, "but I think starting tomorrow you'd better wear it all the time. Whether we're looking for trouble or not, it's going to find us between here and Washington."

"All right."

"Where is your gear?"

"I took a room at the hotel when I came to town. I

guess—I hope—it's still there."

"We'll check and see. If it's still there we'll move it to my room."

"I'm not staying in your room," she said, firmly.

"You can have the bed," he said. "I'll sleep on the floor."

"I'm not sleeping in your room," she said, again, and he could see that she was serious.

"I'm not after your body, Sally—"

"I don't care," she said. "Just because you're guarding me doesn't mean I'm going to give up my privacy. I'm sure we can get rooms right next to each other."

Clint studied the woman across the table and saw that talking her out of this would be a problem, so he decided not to try. Once they got out on the trail and on trains, she wouldn't have much choice in the matter.

After they left the cafe and went to the hotel Clint was able to get the room right next to Sally's.

"I'd suggest you stay in your room the rest of the day," he said, afterward.

"I was better off playing checkers with the deputy at Molly's," she said. "All right, all right, I'm not complaining. I'll stay in my room."

"Good," he said. "I'll be right next door."

She went to her room, and he to his, and after a few hours of staring out the window there was a knock on the door. He had noticed Linda Contact passing through his line of view, and even as the knock sounded on the door he remembered how her hip had pressed against his shoulder while she was serving him, and how her hand had lingered on his arm when they said good-bye.

He went to the door, opened it, and saw that it *was* Linda.

She peered into the room past him and asked, "Alone?"

"As a matter of fact, yes."

She had her hands behind her back and rocked slightly from side to side.

"I like Sally," Linda said, "she's my friend, but she should be more aggressive."

"Like you?"

"Did she warn you about me?"

"Yes," he said, truthfully.

"But you opened the door, anyway," she said. "I saw you at the window, and you saw me."

"I—"

"I expect you'll be leaving in the morning."

"At first light."

"Well," she said, taking her hands out from behind her back, "I was never one to let an opportunity pass. Can I come in?"

Chapter Eight

She let Clint undress her and he removed her shirt first. Her breasts were large and firm, the nipples brown against her fair skin. She had freckles between them and he licked them. She moaned as his mouth moved to one breast, worrying the nipple between his teeth, and then to the other one.

"More clothes," she said.

"What?"

"We've got to get rid of more clothes," she said, pulling his shirt out of his pants.

He helped her with the rest of her clothes, unveiling her wide hips, long legs, and full buttocks. After that she undressed him, pausing to run her hands over his broad chest. She slid his pants down around his ankles and slid her hands over his buttocks, rubbing and squeezing them while nuzzling his rigid cock with her cheek.

With her help he managed to shuck his boots and pants without falling on his head, and they were both finally naked.

They embraced, her breasts mashed against his chest, his massive erection trapped between them, pulsing, their mouths fusing together hungrily. Her tongue shot into his mouth and she moaned and writhed against him. He slid one hand up to cup the back of her neck and the other down to press against the small of her back.

Her hands couldn't seem to decide where they wanted to lay, and finally she just entwined them around his neck, trying to draw herself even closer. Her big body was hot and firm, her flesh smooth and fragrant, and he wasn't surprised at the strength in her arms.

"Am I too heavy?" she asked against his mouth, between wet kisses.

"For what?"

"To do it . . ." she said, kissing him, " . . . standing up?"

To answer her he cupped her buttocks and lifted her. She spread her legs and he impaled her on him. In truth she *was* heavy, but he spread his legs and planted his feet to accommodate her weight and she wrapped her powerful legs around his hips. She began to move her hips and he found her tempo and moved with her.

"Oh God, Clint," she said, throwing her head back, "Oh yes, yes . . ."

A bead of perspiration traveled down the line of her neck and was about to disappear between her breasts when he leaned forward and licked it off. He saw another working its way down her nose, but she licked that one off herself. Seeing her tongue flick out like that inflamed his passion even more. He could feel the strain in his legs from holding her weight, but he also felt the rush in his loins, and soon he was aware of nothing but his cock pumping his seed deep into her in long, powerful, almost painful, spurts.

Chapter Nine

After Linda left there was another knock on the door. This time it was Sally.

"Can I come in?"

"Sure."

She entered and he saw her sniff the air. She looked at the bed, which had obviously been hard used, and she couldn't have helped hearing them since she was right next door, but she said nothing. After all, she *had* warned him about her friend.

"So?" Sally Murcer asked.

"So what?" Clint asked.

"What do you think my chances are?"

"Of reaching Washington alive?"

She nodded and said, "*And* testifying."

"Well, you've got me as an escort, so your chances are very good."

"I'm serious."

"So am I," he said. "I don't know anything about Robert Russell or his men. If the rest of his people are anything like those two in the saloon, then you've got an excellent chance of doing both, arriving *and* testifying. Are all his people loyal to him, no matter what?"

"Aside from one or two, like myself, yes. I didn't realize when I came on that a lot of his people are just hired guns."

"And if he's as wealthy as I've heard, he can afford to hire more."

"Oh, he's wealthy, all right," she said. "Make no mistake about that."

"So there'll be some hired guns after us," Clint said.

"That's right," she said, as if she hadn't thought of that. "Are you worried about that?"

"Sure, I am."

"But you're the Gunsmith," she said. "Surely you're not worried about some hired guns."

"I'd have been dead a long time ago if I *wasn't* worried about hired guns."

She frowned and said, "My chances of surviving are getting slimmer by the minute."

"Look," he said, "if we get you out of this town alive we'll be one up on them. Look at it that way, for now."

"Speaking of which, when are we leaving?"

"First light."

"Don't we need supplies?"

"If I go and buy a lot of supplies everyone will know we're leaving in the morning."

"But you told Ted Winfield we were leaving."

"Is he going to spread that around?"

"I don't think so," she said. "Ted's pretty much his own man."

"Not intimidated by Russell's money?"

"Not that I ever noticed."

Clint wasn't convinced. Ted Winfield had not exactly impressed him.

"Are you ready to tell me where we're heading tomorrow?" she asked.

"No."

"Is there any way I can persuade you?"

Her eyes and face were completely guileless so he resisted the urge to make a joke.

"I don't think so," he said, simply. . . .

Chapter Ten

Clint woke the next morning to a pleasant sensation between his legs. He looked down and saw Linda wrapping her long hair around his penis, and teasing his balls with her nails. She had returned during the night, and he had let her in. Sally Murcer had excited him just by *being* there, and he thought Linda knew that. He also thought, being a very practical woman, that she didn't mind. She *knew*, though—and so did he—that when they were in bed together, he *knew* he was with Linda.

"I thought you'd never wake up," she said, and took him into her mouth.

He wasn't fully erect yet and felt himself growing in her mouth. When he was fully erect she began to suckle him strongly, one hand cupping his balls and the other splayed on his belly. Her head bobbed up and down and he lifted his hips off the bed to meet the suction of her mouth. When she felt that he was ready to explode she slid both hands beneath him to grasp his buttocks tightly. She was digging her sharp nails into him but he didn't feel a thing because he was only aware of her sucking mouth as she accepted his entire emission and tried to milk him for more.

When she released him from her mouth she licked her lips and smiled up at him.

"Time for breakfast?" she asked.

"No breakfast," he said. "Sally and I are getting started in ten minutes. We'll have to have breakfast on the trail."

"Well," she said, sliding up onto his chest, leaning back on her hands, bringing her crotch close to his mouth, "I guess this will have to hold you for a while . . ."

The streets were empty as Clint and Sally made their way to the livery stable. The stable wasn't locked and they went inside and saddled their horses.

"I wish I had time to say good-bye to Molly," Sally said.

"I explained why that wasn't a good idea, Sally," Clint said.

"I know," Sally said, "but I can trust Molly, Clint. I've known her for years."

"It's even safer for her not to know when we left," he said.

"I guess you're right," she said, and then added, "and even if you're not, you're in charge. I guess I've got to do as you say."

Clint wondered how long *that* attitude would last.

When they rode out of Wells, Arizona, the sun was just starting to rise.

Chapter Eleven

Without being physically large, Robert Russell was an imposing figure. A dapper man of only about five-seven, he nevertheless had a magnetism that commanded respect and—as in the case of his lawyer—fear.

Phillip Gordon was also a small man, barely five-and-a-half-feet tall, who sometimes thought that his most important qualification for his job was that he was almost an inch shorter than Russell. He'd worked for Robert Russell for almost eight years.

They were in Robert Russell's office on K Street in Washington, D.C. Off to one side was a tray of cold food that Russell had ordered for breakfast, and then promptly forgotten about.

"Come on, Gordon," Russell said now. "Where is the girl?"

Gordon fidgeted uncomfortably and admitted, "We don't know."

"What do you mean, you don't know? Is she still in Wells?"

"A man rode into town yesterday and took her out of the rooming house, where we had her spotted."

"And?"

"He took her to the hotel."

"Don't make me drag this out of you, Phillip."

"They disappeared the next morning, Mr. Russell. We're looking for them now."

"Who was the man?"

"According to my sources," Gordon said, "his name is Clint Adams."

"Adams?" Russell said. "The goddamned Gunsmith?"

"That's the man."

"And he took her out of town?"

"Yes."

"Without being seen?"

"Apparently."

Russell considered briefly what good it would do him to threaten Phillip Gordon. He decided that it would be a waste of time. The man couldn't possibly be more frightened of him than he already was.

"Where is Stark?"

"He hasn't arrived yet," Gordon said. "He should be here later this afternoon."

That annoyed Russell. He'd given the hired killer, Stark, plenty of work in the past. The least the man could do was come as soon as he was called.

"When he gets here bring him right to me."

"We, uh, might be in court, Mr.—"

"Then have him brought directly here," Russell said, wearily. "I'm going to want to talk to him as soon as I return."

"Yes, sir. I'll see to it."

"Now get out, Gordon," Russell said. "I want to be alone."

"Yes, sir."

After the little attorney left, Russell stood up and looked out the window at the street below. If that bitch Sally Murcer made it to Washington she could bring down everything he had built. What had ever possessed him to even *hire* a woman as a ranch hand? They were born busybodies, all of them. If she hadn't been so goddamned attractive—*and* she had the nerve to rebuff his amorous advances.

She'd pay for *that*, if for nothing else.

Chapter Twelve

The initial travel day went easily. Clint kept an eye on their back trail and saw no indication that they were being followed.

"I'm starting to get hungry," Sally said at one point.

"I don't want to stop anywhere today," Clint said. "I have some beef jerky you can munch on."

He handed her a piece, which she chewed without enthusiasm.

"Why can't we stop?"

"I want to put some distance between us and Wells before I make a stop," he explained, "just to be on the safe side."

She didn't argue with him and he liked her more for it. She did, however, ask, "When are we going to stop to eat?"

"Soon."

"What are we going to eat? We can't just eat beef jerky."

"We'll catch something."

"Catch something?"

"A rabbit, maybe some fish."

"There is a stream a couple of hours from here—"

"Good, we'll head there."

"—but what will you use to catch fish with?"

"Wait and see."

The rode on for almost two hours and finally came to the stream.

"Take care of the horses," he told her, "and start a fire."

"What are you going to do?"

"Some fishing."

While she took care of the horses Clint unwound some thread from the bottom of his pants, then went back to his horse to dig into his saddlebags.

"What are you looking for?" Sally asked.

"This," Clint said, showing her a sewing needle.

He poked the thread through the eye of the needle on the first try and then knotted it. She had picketed the horses and started collecting the makings for a fire.

Clint began poking around near the bank of the stream, hoping to find a nice juicy worm. When he didn't he moved away from the stream to where there was some foliage. Poking around in there he finally found something that would work. It was a grasshopper. Not the best kind of bait, but it would have to do.

It took only about twenty minutes—after Clint had pulled in his line two or three more times—that something finally hit the line.

He walked to the edge of the stream so that when he pulled in his fish he could grab ahold if it before it could slip away from the needle. When he did take hold of the fish it almost slipped from his grasp. He got a good two-handed grip on it and carried it back to where Sally was making coffee.

"I've got a frying pan in my saddlebags," he told her. "Why don't you go and get it?"

While she did that he gutted the fish, cleaned and scaled it, and cut off the head and the tail. He had done some fishing, but was no expert on fish. He was glad she hadn't asked him what kind it was. All he knew was that he wanted to eat it.

"Why don't you take off those wet boots and socks?" she said when they sat down to eat. He did so, and she laid the socks out on a rock.

"That was nice of you," he said.

"I don't want my bodyguard dying of pneumonia before you get me where I have to go."

When they had finished eating Sally cleaned the plates while Clint put on a second pot of coffee. It was dark when she settled across from him, on the other side of the fire.

She had cleaned up without being told. She had also unsaddled the horses and picketed them instead of waiting for him to do it.

He liked her for that. She wasn't going to be a helpless female through all this, and for that he was glad.

Without even trying she had made him start to like her enough so that keeping her alive was going to become something personal.

Chapter Thirteen

Del Stark knew Robert Russell's type well, which is the reason he waited three days before finally letting Russell—through the attorney, Gordon—know that he was in town. Russell expected the people he employed to jump when he said jump. He expected them to be afraid of him.

Stark and Russell knew each other well. They knew each other's *type* well. Still, Stark always felt compelled to send Russell a message when the man sent for him. He always responded late to a summons from Robert Russell. He felt that was enough to tell the rich man that Del Stark was not afraid of him simply because he had money.

Del Stark was for sale, that was true, but he was afraid of no one. That was something he had taken great pains over the years to make sure people knew.

Stark was sitting across the desk from Phillip Gordon in the lawyer's office. He had been dealing with the little lawyer for as long as he had been dealing with Russell. The lawyer obviously feared Stark. Stark enjoyed watching the droplets of sweat run down the little lawyer's face and neck into his collar.

"Mr. Russell expected you earlier," Gordon said.

"I'm here now," Stark said.

"We'll have to go to his office to see him," Gordon said. "We were in court this morning."

Stark wasn't interested in *why* they were in court anymore than he was interested in the fact that they *were* in court. It didn't make a difference to him what Russell was doing, unless it had some bearing on him directly.

"Can we go now?" Stark asked.

"Oh, uh, sure."

Gordon rose from the desk and started around it. When he saw that this would take him very near the killer he turned and walked the other way. His fear of the man seemed to increase the closer he got to him. For that reason he tried to keep the man at more than an arm's length when they had dealings—which was too often to suit Gordon.

It never got any easier.

When Stark and Gordon entered Russell's hotel room, Russell immediately said, "That's all, Phillip. You can leave."

The little lawyer left the room quickly, thankful for the opportunity.

"Have a seat," Russell said to Stark.

"I'll stand."

"Where the hell have you been?" Russell said, snarling.

"Sorry?"

"I sent for you days ago."

They went through this ritual every time, Russell pretending that he was incensed at having been kept waiting.

"You are not the only man who employs me, Mr. Russell," was all Stark would say, and he said it calmly.

It infuriated Russell when Stark treated him this way, but what could he realistically do about it? The man was a killer, which was what he paid him for, but what if Stark ever decided he didn't *need* Russell's money anymore? Russell made a mental note to see about hiring someone who might be able to handle Stark when that time came.

"All right," Russell said, "all right . . . well, you're here now."

"Yes."

"Do you know who Clint Adams is?"

Stark sat forward in his chair so abruptly that Russell sat back in his, even though the wide expanse of his desk was separating them.

"The Gunsmith?"

"That's right."

"What about him."

"Do you think you can take him?"

"Is that the job?" Stark asked. Russell thought he detected a note of eagerness in the man's voice.

"I'll tell you about the job," Russell said, sensing that *he* now had the upper hand on the killer, "but first, maybe you like some coffee . . ."

Chapter Fourteen

"That's Amberville," Sally Murcer said. "There's only about twenty people or so still living there."

"Has it got a general store?" Clint asked.

"Sure," she said. "People pass through all the time, but nobody ever stays."

"Why not?"

She looked at him and said, "Everybody who lives there is crazy." She didn't explain any further.

"That's where we'll stock up, then."

"Uh, Clint, do we really have to go down there?" she asked.

"We need supplies," Clint said, "and the horses can rest."

"We're not going to spend the night there?" she called after him as he rode ahead.

• • •

Somehow Robert Russell's office seemed cleaner, the air fresher, after the killer, Stark, had left. Russell knew that he had bent the law over and over during his climb to the top, but he somehow felt that he was cleaner than Stark. At least *he* had never killed anyone—at least, not with his own hands.

He poured himself a brandy and lit a cigar. The morning in court had been a formality, a reading of the charges. The government was really out to nail him this time, but their entire case hinged on the girl—and there wasn't a chance in hell of her getting to Washington alive. And even if she did, Stark would be waiting.

The Gunsmith, Del Stark thought as he left Russell's room. He knew he had agreed to this job for a lot less than Russell would have paid, but if he could kill the Gunsmith it would *make* his reputation.

Some things were more important than money.

The man standing across the street watched Del Stark as he walked away from the building, then stepped from his doorway to follow him. Once he knew where Stark was staying, he'd report back to William Masters Cartwright.

Cartwright had predicted correctly.

Stark was in Washington, and that meant somebody was going to die.

As Clint and Sally rode into Amberville there was dust everywhere. There was also some foliage growing up through the floorboards of the boardwalks, and even out some of the windows.

"There's the general store," Clint said. "I hope there's someone there."

"So do I."

They dismounted in front of the place, tied the horses off, and went inside.

"Jesus," Sally said, inside.

Dust was very much in evidence here, too, but there were some clean areas—relatively clean, that is—on the counter, so Clint walked up to it and pounded on it.

"Anyone here?"

There was no answer.

"Well," he said, examining the walls and the shelves, "it's not well stocked, but there are some things we need. Flour, coffee, sugar, canned goods."

"No meats?" Sally asked, disappointed.

"If there were meats here they'd be green," he said. "Let's gather some of this stuff together while we wait for the owner."

They started to do that when a man stepped through the curtained doorway behind the counter and trained a gun on them. He was a man in his mid-forties who probably, under normal circumstances, had an open, pleasant face. At the moment his face was grimly set.

"Can I help you folks?"

"We just need some supplies," Clint said. "There's no need for the gun."

"Can't be too careful hereabouts," the man said. "You've both heard the stories."

"About what?" Clint asked.

"About everyone here being crazy," he said. "Well, I'm sorry to disappoint you, but I'm as sane as either one of you, but people usually think they can come in here and take what they want without paying."

"We intended to pay," Clint said. "We were just collecting the supplies until we could find someone *to* pay."

"That'd be me," the man said. He put the gun down underneath the counter, within easy reach, then extended his hand to Clint and said, "Sam Castle."

Clint took the man's hand and said, "Clint Adams." He deliberately did not introduce Sally.

Castle had a powerful grip and although he had a huge belly, Clint knew that there was a lot of power in the man, and no fat.

"We didn't mean any disrespect—" Clint started.

"We're awful sorry, we didn't—" Sally said in unison with Clint.

Castle raised his hands and said, "Please, there's no need to apologize. Just collect what you need and I'll tally it up."

Clint and Sally went about doing just that, and brought everything back to the counter.

"Why do you stay here?" Sally asked.

"Where would I go?" Castle asked. "This is my home. A lot of us who are left feel the same way. We've just got nowhere else to go. Now, what else can I do for you folks?"

"You haven't got much here to keep you . . ." Clint said, sadly.

"And when this is gone," he said, indicating the stock in the store with a sweep of one powerful arm, "that'll be the end of the general store and I'll close it down. I'm sorry I don't have any of the latest conveniences—"

"We were just hoping for some meat," Sally said.

"Sorry, can't help you there. You seem to have here just about all I can offer you, unless you want some clothes, or a hat?"

"We'll take a bag of candy," Clint said.

"What for?" Sally asked.

"Never mind," Clint said to Sam.

"All right, then, that'll be three dollars."

"That's all?" Clint thought. "For all this?"

"It's enough," Castle said. "Where am I going to spend it?"

"You've got a point there," Clint said, and paid the man.

Outside they stuffed both their saddlebags with the supplies and then mounted up.

"Let's get out of here," Sally said. "I don't want to meet any of the other citizens of Amberville."

Clint didn't argue. He felt the same way.

Chapter Fifteen

A full day's ride behind them, three men were riding together, and they were arguing.

"This is useless," one man said. "We're so far behind them now—"

"You want to tell Mr. Russell that we let them get away?" the third man asked. His name was Luger, Lex Luger, and he was a big man with a deep chest and broad shoulders. His arms had biceps like cannonballs, and his fists were like sledgehammers.

The other two men were Sid Vinton and Scott Long. They were the two men who had encountered Clint in the saloon the day he arrived in Wells.

Lex Luger said, "If you two idiots had killed this man in the saloon—"

"We explained that," Sid Vinton said, "he got the jump on us, Lex."

"Yeah," Scott Long said, backing up his partner's story.

Luger was technically the foreman of Russell's ranch, but he knew nothing about ranching. He knew how to handle men, though, like these two.

Long looked at Vinton and said, "If that damned bartender had backed us—"

"Forget it," Luger said. "I'll take care of them myself when we catch up to them."

"You really think we're gonna catch them?" Long asked.

"I wouldn't be out here if I didn't," Luger said. "Now stop yapping, both of you. You're givin' me a damned headache."

Luger had sent out other two and three men search parties to look for Clint Adams and Sally Murcer. They had fanned out in every direction from Wells, but Luger felt certain that he, Long, and Vinton had found the real trail. Now that they were following it, though, Luger wished he had better men with him than these two.

Chapter Sixteen

Clint and Sally were camped for the night, and Clint had opened up some canned fruit for their dinner. Sally knew they couldn't hunt because they'd have to fire their guns, thus bringing attention to themselves.

"Sally, if you want me to wrestle a bear for you," Clint said, "you're going to have to do more than just say please."

She looked down and said, "Well, these peaches aren't all *that* bad . . ."

"Don't make fun of the cook, Sally," Clint said, warning her. "Can you do any better?"

"Hell, no," she said. "I'm a terrible cook . . ."

"I'll clean the plates tonight."

"And I suppose I have to take first watch?"

Clint had set the watches the first night on the

trail, telling her that he'd take the first because she had cleaned the plates. She had made an issue of it that first night, claiming that she could keep watch just as well as he could, until he agreed that they'd alternate watches.

"Yep," he said now, "the first watch is yours."

She took the first watch, annoyed with her reaction to his remark about having to say more than please. It had embarrassed her. The truth was, she would have liked to do more than say please, but she didn't know how. She wasn't as aggressive as her friend Linda was. She knew how to handle cows, and cow*hands*, but when it actually came to dealing with a man she was attracted to, Sally Murcer was helpless.

In Washington Robert Russell was having a dinner that consisted of a sixteen-ounce steak, vegetables, soft rolls, wine, and coffee. When he was done he lit a cigar without offering one to Phillip Gordon and then addressed the little lawyer, who had watched his boss eat.

"Tell me what went on in court today," Russell said to Gordon.

"It's simple. They're using delaying tactics, trying to slow things down until their witness arrives."

Russell smiled.

"Won't they be surprised when she doesn't show up?"

"Er, about that—"

"Never mind about that," Russell said. "What did you find out about this Clint Adams?"

"Plenty," Gordon said. He took something from his

pocket and tossed it on the table between them. Russell saw that it was a dime novel. "Out West they call him the Gunsmith. He's something of a legend."

"Then what we have heard *is* true?" Russell asked. "The man is for real and not the result of some dime novelist's imagination?"

"Partly," Gordon said. "Legends are usually more exaggeration than truth, but I think it's safe to say that the man is dangerous."

"So is the man I hired," Russell said. "This will make it more interesting for Stark. We wouldn't want our hired killer getting bored, would we, Gordon?"

"Uh, no, sir." Gordon was frowning, wondering just who it was going to be more interesting for.

"All right, you can go, Gordon. I'm going to finish this cigar, read a little of this book, and then go to sleep. Sitting around all day watching you fence with their lawyers is tiring work."

"Yes, sir," Gordon said, and left.

While Clint and Sally camped, Lex Luger had his two men moving with him through the night.

"We're gonna get killed moving around out here at night," Sid Vinton complained.

"I know this country like nobody else," Lex Luger said. "I can travel in the dark. All you have to do is follow me."

"Follow you," Vinton said, huffing. He looked at Long, who looked back and shrugged.

Lex Luger's mind was not on the complaints of Long and Vinton, but on the girl they were chasing. There was a big bonus offered for the girl, and he was going to collect it, even if he did have to go up against the Gunsmith.

And he had no intention of sharing.

William Masters Cartwright was beside himself. He was angry that he had not heard from Clint Adams.

The plan had been for Adams to check in every two days, but Cartwright should have known that Adams would change oars in the water. It was infuriating to have to deal with the man. He had no respect for authority, and insisted on doing things his own way. Cartwright already *had* a man like that working for him in Jim West, and he didn't need another.

He felt sure that Adams and the girl were still alive at this point. Adams was simply playing his cards close to the vest. Cartwright was just going to have to sit back and wait to see if Adams got the woman to Washington. He was sure that Robert Russell was doing the same thing.

If Adams managed to keep the girl alive long enough to get her to Washington Cartwright knew that Russell would be waiting for them—that is, he'd have *killers* waiting for them. Cartwright was going to have men covering the railroad station, and he just hoped that they'd be able to avoid a wild gun battle between agents and killers.

Chapter Seventeen

At breakfast Clint decided to tell Sally where they were heading.

"Denver," he said.

"Denver?" she asked. "Why there?"

"The railroad," he said.

"Does the train go to Washington from there?"

"No. We'll have to take a train to Chicago, and then take one from there to Washington."

"Chicago?" she said. "I've never been East, Clint. What's Chicago like?"

"Big," he said.

"And Washington?"

"The same."

"And I've never been to Denver," she said. "What's Denver like?"

"You'll see when we get there."

"This is very exciting, you know," Sally said. "I

mean, if I live through this and get to go to all those places, it'll be very . . . exciting."

"You'll live through it, Sally."

"Clint," she said, after a moment, "won't they expect us to take the railroad?"

"They probably will," he said, "but it's still the fastest way to get you to Washington. If we tried to ride the whole way we'd be at risk from ambush every day we were on the trail."

"Won't we be in danger in Denver? And on the train?"

"Sure we will," he said, "but at least we won't be out in the open. In the city, and on the train, there'll be plenty of places for cover."

She shivered a bit, as if she was cold, and said, "I never thought about what it would be like to be hunted. It's horrible."

"The quicker we get to Washington," he said, "the quicker it will be over."

"Then by all means," she said, "let's take the train."

"Do we have the train station covered?" Robert Russell asked Phillip Gordon.

They were in Russell's office, conducting some business that had nothing to do with the government case against him. Just because he was in Washington under indictment didn't mean that Russell was going to let all of his businesses suffer. They had finished discussing his other businesses—both legal and illegal—and now they were discussing the pressing matters of the moment.

"Yes," Gordon said. "I have men watching the train station—"

"I want some other train stations covered, as well," he said.

"Uh, which ones?"

"Denver and Chicago," Russell said.

"Why?"

Russell grinned at Gordon.

"Because if it was my job to keep that woman alive I'd head for Denver. You're not going to ride a horse all the way here, and Denver is the largest city that he can ride to with access to the East." Russell touched the end of his pencil to his chin. "He'll take a train from Denver to Chicago, figuring that crowds at both ends will keep them from being seen."

"Mr. Russell, won't Adams know all of that?" Gordon asked. "Won't he stay away from those places?"

"I don't think so," Russell said. "He's going to want to get the woman here the fastest way possible, and that means using the trains. Don't you agree?"

"I suppose so, sir."

"That's good, Phillip," Russell said, "that's very good. I want to be able to feel that I can count on you."

"You can."

"Then you will take care of this matter of the train stations."

"I will, sir."

"Now."

"Right now?" Gordon asked. "We have a lot of work to go over—"

"I can go over this material while you're gone, Phillip," Russell said. "You have a lot of telegrams to send."

Gordon frowned and was tempted to argue further, but thought better of it. If Robert Russell wanted to let his other enterprises suffer, that was his business.

"Go and do what I told you, Gordon," Russell said. "When you return, I'll be prepared to discuss some of this other material with you."

"As you wish," Phillip Gordon said.

Russell had already turned his attention back to the paper before Gordon even reached the door.

"I hate this place," Scott Long said.

He was speaking of Amberville.

"You've been here before?" Lex Luger asked.

"Once," Long said. "There were more people then, and they were crazy."

"There doesn't seem to be many people here," said Luger.

"Believe me, the people who are here are nuts. They say this town is haunted, too."

"Can't be haunted if there's still people living in it," Luger said. "That's a lot of bull. Let's go into the general store. If they came through here they must have stopped there."

They all dismounted and entered the store, and the man behind the counter looked up.

"What can I do for you, fellas?" the man asked. "I don't have very much—"

"We're looking for some information," Lex Luger said.

"What kind of information?"

"We're looking for a man and a woman traveling together."

"What do you mean traveling together?"

"The woman you can't miss," Luger said, ignoring

the man's question. "She's tall and has red hair, she's a real beauty, that bitch is."

"What do you want them for?"

"We don't know much about the man except that he's tall and dark-haired." Luger continued to ignore the man's questions.

"I asked you—"

Luger's big hand came up and closed on the man's throat.

"I heard you, friend," he said, squeezing. "If I wanted to answer your questions I would have. Now, answer *my* question!" He put his gun against the man's forehead. "Did you see the man and the woman pass through here?"

Chapter Eighteen

Sally Murcer was completely awed by Denver. She'd never seen so many people and so many big buildings in one place before, and the fact that some of the streets were cobblestones and not dirt fascinated her. She reacted to the city as if she was twelve years old.

"And look at the way the women dress," she said, eyeing the women who were walking on the street.

"We'll get settled in a hotel and then buy you some new clothes—after I check the railroad schedules."

"All right."

They left their horses at the livery. Clint made a deal with the liveryman. He could have Sally's horse if he took good care of Duke until he came back for it. Luckily, Sally's horse was young and strong enough that the man saw it as a good deal. Clint was perfectly willing to leave Sally's horse behind, but Duke was coming the whole way with him. He wasn't about to leave the big gelding behind.

After that they went to a hotel that Clint knew of. It was not a large, fancy hotel, but it was still much more opulent than anything Sally had seen.

"This hotel is still much better than anything I've ever been in. Will we be getting one room?"

"Unless you have some objections, this time," he said, reminding her that she had objected back in Wells.

"No," she said, looking sheepish, "no argument this time, Clint."

To make it up to her for not taking her to one of the larger hotels, Clint asked for a suite. Cartwright was picking up the tab, so why not?

When they entered the suite she couldn't believe it.

"It's beautiful," she said, looking around at the stuffed furniture and brocade drapes. "And there's another room, with a bed," she went on, exploring further.

"And a good lock on the door," he said, locking it behind them. "You're going to stay here while I go to the railroad station. Keep the door locked and your gun handy, Sally."

"There's a bathtub!"

He showed her how to fill the bathtub and she was fascinated by that, as well. She was so wide-eyed that Clint had to make sure he had her full attention.

"Now, listen good. Keep the door locked and your gun near you, even in the tub. Understand?"

"Yes, sir," she said, with mock severity.

"This is no joke, Sally."

"You don't think I know that?" she asked.

"Keep the door locked until I get back."

"Be careful."

He smiled and said, "I'm always careful."

He went to the door, unlocked it, then turned back to her and said, "Remember, keep it locked and don't let anyone in."

"I'll tell all my men callers to come back another time," she said.

It looked as if Sally Murcer was beginning to loosen up. To him, it was an admirable reaction to the pressure she was under.

He didn't like the idea of leaving her alone but that damned red hair made her stand out so much—not that the rest of her wasn't attention-getting, as well.

Clint knew he could have gotten in touch with any number of people he knew in Denver who could help them. Talbot Roper, for one. Even Allan Pinkerton, but he decided not to let *anyone* know that he was there.

Clint went to the railroad station and meandered about for a while, trying to see if there was anyone watching the place. A man as wealthy as Robert Russell was bound to have contacts in a city the size of Denver. When he was reasonably sure that there wasn't he went up to one of the clerks and asked for a schedule. He folded it and put it in his pocket. He'd check it out back at the hotel. He wanted to get off the streets because he had no way of knowing if his description had been circulated.

He hurried back to the hotel. If Sally was finished with her bath they'd go out and buy her some clothes, shopping someplace close to the hotel.

As Clint Adams left the train station Frank Conrad entered it from another direction. Conrad was a private investigator who worked the cases operators like Allan Pinkerton and Talbot Roper wouldn't work. That meant that he worked for people like Robert Russell, people who needed to have the law bent for their benefit. If they paid Conrad enough, then he went ahead and bent the law.

He was a man of medium height and maximum girth. From an early age he knew that he'd always be fat, so he made a point of making enough money so that he could *dress* his fat well. He pampered himself with expensive clothes and expensive whores. This was all the more reason he had to work for men like Robert Russell.

He made a circuit around the station and didn't see a tall, red-haired woman. He asked the clerks if *they* had seen a beautiful red-haired woman, and didn't bother asking them about a tall, dark-haired man. It was the woman who would stand out in the minds of the men who saw her. Her companion—if she was anywhere as lovely as he'd been led to believe—would go virtually unnoticed.

Conrad was satisfied that the man and woman weren't there now and hadn't been there yet—at least, not together. Now he took a seat and waited for the two men he was going to hire to help him on this assignment. They'd be cheap labor, guns with no brains, and that was what he wanted for this piece of business.

Frank Conrad had a habit of hiring men who were capable of doing what they were told and who would never in a million years formulate an original thought of their own.

Chapter Nineteen

While Clint Adams was gone Sally Murcer luxuri-
ated in a hot bath. She had put her flaming red hair
up, and had her gun hanging on the back of a chair
that stood right next to the tub.

Lying in the tub, rubbing herself with a washcloth,
she thought about Clint Adams. He was easily the
most interesting man she had ever met, and the most
attractive. It was obvious to her that he was also
attracted to her. That wasn't hard to see, in the way
he looked at her.

She warned herself not to get too serious about
him, though. She was also sure that he was a man
who would resist being tied down. Still, having a ca-
sual relationship with him was something she found
exciting, but something she wasn't sure she'd be able
to do.

When she heard the noise at the door she reached for her gun without shaking the soapsuds off her hand first. The gun squirted from her grip and hit the floor just as Clint Adams entered.

"I guess we'll have to work out some kind of signal," he said, smiling at her.

They left the hotel but stayed within easy walking distance. They both needed some new clothes, and since the government would be paying he didn't worry too much about price. When they were done Sally wanted to go back to the hotel and try on the clothes they had bought. She wanted to show off for him.

Clint knew she was excited, so he didn't mind sitting still and letting her model the clothes for him.

Sally had been wondering all day long how to get him to make another advance at her. She had decided that she would respond to his next one. She remembered Linda always telling her she should be more aggressive when she saw a man she liked, but she hadn't seen many men she was attracted to.

As she removed the last dress she wondered what Linda would do now if she wanted to make love with Clint Adams.

That was easy.

When she stepped out from behind the screen, naked, she was almost as surprised as Clint Adams was.

They made love, both surprised at how hungry for it they both were.

She took the top the first time, riding him vigor-

ously while he squeezed her breasts in his hands
and sucked her nipples. Her breasts were full and
firm, with wide, light-brown nipples and aureola,
and heavy undersides. Her skin was incredibly clear
and smooth, almost like glass. Her body was much
like Linda's, but longer, more firmly toned than the
older woman's. She was not as skillful as Linda was,
but she made up for it with eagerness.

He turned her over after that, assuming the top
position himself, and took her with long, deep, easy
strokes. At least, they *started* out as easy strokes, but
soon he was increasing the tempo, and she was urging
him on, saying, "harder . . . faster . . . ooh, yes, Clint,
please . . ."

She wrapped her hands in the bedsheet as he
pounded into her, her legs wrapped around him
tightly, and when she came she arched her back
and lifted them both off the bed with amazing
strength.

"I was jealous of Linda back in Wells, you know,"
she said.

"You were?"

"Uh-huh." She burrowed close to him, and he put
his arm around and let his hand rest lightly on her
breast. "She's always been more aggressive than I
have, she's always trying to get me to go after something I want."

"Which you did this time, right?"

"Right," she said, kissing his right nipple, "but that
was more because of you than because of her."

"I'm flattered."

"I'm hungry."

"We could go downstairs . . ."

"No," she said, sliding her hand down over his belly, "not *that* kind of hungry . . ."

They made love again, and after that they *both* experienced the other kind of hunger.

Chapter Twenty

They went down to the hotel dining room for dinner, and while it was smaller than a lot of hotel dining rooms Clint had been inside in other hotels in Denver, or San Francisco, Sally was excited by it.

The waiters were well dressed and polite, and their particular waiter was so enamored of Sally's beauty that he gave them extra special service.

"It must be that dress," Clint said.

Two of the dresses they had bought her were for everyday wear, but Clint had wanted to do something nice for her, so they bought one dress that she could wear out to dinner. She had worn it tonight, and Clint had worn his new suit.

It was green, a marvelous color for her, and low cut enough to show the creamy valley between her full breasts.

After dinner they ordered dessert, and then Clint signed the check and they left the dining room to go back to their room.

"Could we go for a walk?" she asked. She had a shawl that they had bought and wrapped it snugly around her shoulders.

"That wouldn't be wise."

"Why not?" she asked. "Nobody knows we're here yet. We're not being watched, are we?"

"Not that I can tell."

"Then what harm would a walk do?"

"Sally—"

"Please? Just a short walk?"

It was amazing that a woman as robust as she was could project such a little girl quality when she wanted to.

"All right," he said, "a short walk."

"Thank you," she said, kissing him on the cheek.

They left the hotel and started walking down the paved sidewalk.

"I've never seen a place as lit up at night as this city."

"You should see San Francisco," he said.

"I'd like to, some day."

"Chicago will be like this," he said. "Somewhat colder, but like this."

"When will we leave?"

He was about to answer when he became aware of footsteps behind them, footsteps he should have heard sooner.

"Move!" he said, pushing Sally away from him just as he received a blow to the middle of his back, which knocked him to the ground.

As a man leaned over him Clint drew his gun from his belt, where he'd tucked it earlier, and pistol-whipped the fella on the side of the head. The man fell on him, and he struggled to get out from under the dead weight so he could check on Sally.

He finally got the man off him and as he rose he saw the second man and Sally struggling for her bag. Suddenly, she released it and swung her fist at the man, connecting with his jaw.

"Ow!" the man shouted in surprise. "Let's get out of here!"

As the men ran off Clint moved to Sally and took hold of her shoulders. "Are you all right?"

"I'm fine," she said.

The commotion had attracted some attention and people were starting to respond.

"Let's get out of here before the police arrive," he said, pushing her toward the hotel.

"Why? We didn't do anything wrong."

"We don't need the extra attention," Clint said. "Besides, a man like Robert Russell has to have somebody in the police department on his payroll."

"You think his influence is that far ranging?" she asked.

"How wealthy is he?"

"Very."

"Then the answer is yes. Come on, let's get back to the hotel."

Chapter Twenty-One

When they got back to their room Sally said, "Look at your hands."

Clint looked down and saw that his hands were scraped, not raw, but enough for many little pinpricks of blood to be showing. She got some water and a cloth to clean his hands.

"I could have gotten both of us killed for nothing," she said, scolding herself. "There are enough people around who would do it for a reason without me risking our lives for nothing."

"Don't worry about it. How's your dress?"

She examined her new dress and pronounced it fit.

"What about your suit?"

He checked himself out and found an abrasion in the material on one knee.

"It's fine," he said, "but I'd better change."

The incident on the street seemed to have drained her of some of her little girl awe and brought her back to reality.

That was good, he thought, because when your life was in danger you needed to have both feet firmly planted on the ground.

"I have a better idea," she said, and started to remove her dress.

They went to bed and made love again. They needed it after the scare on the street. Unmindful of the scrapes on his hands and knees Clint entered her and quickly pounded his way to release for *both* of them.

Afterward they checked the railroad schedule. She leaned on him while they both read it, and he was acutely aware of her breasts pressing into his back.

Clint decided to go out the next morning and get them tickets on an afternoon train to Chicago. That done, he put the schedule on the table near the bed and got up.

"Where are you going?"

"To check the door," he said, "and to set out some alarms."

"Alarms?" she asked, slipping from the bed and following him.

She watched with interest as he checked the lock on the front door and then wedged a straight-backed chair beneath the doorknob. Next he went to the window and set the water pitcher on it so that if the window opened and someone tried to get in he would knock it off. Even if it didn't break, it would make a racket.

In the bedroom he did the same thing, using the bowl from the pitcher and bowl set to prepare the bedroom window in the same manner.

"We should be able to get some sleep now," he said.

He turned and she was so close behind him that he bumped into her. It was a pleasure bumping into someone who had the contours that she had.

"That is," he said, putting his arms around her, "if we feel like getting any sleep."

She laughed and was still laughing when he covered her mouth with his.

Frank Conrad had stationed his two men at the train station, and then had recruited some street urchins for another job.

The boys who roamed and lived on the streets were the cheapest labor he could find, but they were also reliable. He usually used boys from ten to fifteen years old, boys who would do almost anything for two bits.

He collected about a dozen of them and then gave them each the name of a hotel to watch. When they asked what they were watching for he told them a beautiful red-haired woman, alone or in the company of a tall dark-haired man. He promised a dollar to the boy who spotted them, and they went to it, eagerly.

Now Conrad was waiting in his office. He had heard from nine of the urchins, and none of them had seen the red-haired woman.

Finally, the tenth boy came into his office with good news.

"I seen her," he said.

"Are you sure?"

"I'm real sure," the boy said. He was older than the others, thirteen or fourteen.

"All right," Conrad said, shaking his head. "Was there a man with her?"

"Yup, big, tall man with a gun."

"A gun?"

"And he hit a man with it."

"Tell me about that," Frank Conrad said, with interest. After the boy told his story Conrad asked, "Did they wait for a policeman?"

"Nope, they got out of there quick."

"And what hotel was this?"

The boy gave him the name of the hotel, and the street it was on.

"All right," Conrad said. He dug in his pocket and came up with a dollar. "Here, you earned this."

"Thanks, mister," the boy said, clutching the money in a grimy paw.

"Now get out of here," Conrad told him. "If I need you again I know where to find you."

"Sure, mister," the boy said. "You need me again you just let me know."

After the boy left Conrad closed up his office and left, sure that the boy had given him the right information. How many red-haired women like that could there be in town?

He went home to go to bed, because he would be up bright and early and be watching that hotel, himself. He wasn't going to depend on anyone else when he was obviously this close.

Chapter Twenty-Two

Clint leaned over and kissed Sally on the mouth. She shifted, muttered something, but didn't wake up. He took her lower lip between his lips and sucked on it. At the same time he slid his hand over her smooth belly and tangled his fingers in her pubic hair. His middle finger just teased her a bit.

"Mmmph," she said, sleepily, moving her hips.

"I'm going out," he said, releasing her lip.

"What time is it?"

"It's early, just after eight. I want to get to the station and back while the streets are still relatively empty."

He started to move away from her and she put her arms around his neck, holding him tightly.

"Oh no, no, no," she said, "you can't wake me like that and then just walk away."

"I can't?" he asked.

"No," she said, pulling him down to her, "you can't."

She kissed him hungrily, thrusting her tongue into his mouth, and he slid his hands beneath her firm, solid buttocks, lifted her and entered her cleanly and swiftly. She gasped into his mouth, then wrapped her arms around him and lifted her hips to meet his anxious thrusts. . . .

Frank Conrad had been in the doorway across from the St. Martin's Hotel since six-thirty. He'd wanted to get there by six, but Kathy—the whore he had taken home for the night—had other ideas about that, and five minutes had stretched into thirty.

He was getting too fond of Kathy—flat chest, narrow hips, big nose, and all. It might just be time to cut her loose and send her back to the herd. She was good with him, almost made him feel like she *wanted* to be with him, but he knew that was because he paid her well.

He was still thinking about her when he saw the tall, dark-haired man come out of the hotel. Conrad shifted back into the shadows as the man looked up and down the street, and then started to walk north.

Conrad had no doubt that the man was going to the railroad station. Rather than follow him there, he took a shortcut and got there ahead of him.

When Clint got to the train station there were a few people already there. He went up to one of the clerks and bought two tickets to Chicago. The exchange took only a few moments, and when he turned away from the window he thought he saw a man watching him.

He put the tickets in his pocket and walked out of the station.

Frank Conrad wasn't sure where this man—Clint Adams, if he was following the right man—would be going now, so he had to follow him this time. He'd keep a safe and discreet distance so that the man wouldn't catch on.

Of course, he knew he could have been following the wrong man, but this fella fit the description of the famous Gunsmith, and he had come out of the right hotel. Conrad knew he had to make a decision, so he decided that he was on the right trail.

Clint spotted the man following him after he'd gone a few blocks. He'd had the feeling that he was being watched since leaving the hotel, but this was the first time he'd been able to spot the man. He used the window of a store to check and make sure and was now sure that the corpulent yet well-dressed man had followed him from the train station. He wondered why the man dressed so distinctly if he was going to be following someone. It sure didn't help him blend into the background—especially at this hour of the morning, when there was hardly any background to blend into.

The streets were still fairly empty, and Clint didn't blame the man for being spotted. It was hard trying to follow someone on an empty street.

And it was going to be just as hard to lose someone.

Conrad figured he'd been spotted, but he stuck with it. He knew that his size made it difficult to follow someone without being seen, and the streets being so empty didn't help. It was too early and he'd dressed wrong for tailing someone, discreet distance or no. He would just have to keep at it and see how Clint Adams reacted.

Clint Adams knew Denver fairly well. He had been there enough times to know where hotels and restaurants were, but he didn't know the streets well enough to lose the man trailing him, especially if the man himself *lived* in Denver.

Clint turned right at the next corner, not having the faintest idea where he was going.

Frank Conrad had it figured now. The other man didn't know where he was going, but he knew he was being followed.

Conrad did the only thing he could think of to avoid a long walk to nowhere. He broke off and headed for the man's hotel. If Adams thought he'd lost him, that's where he'd head for.

Clint made another right and then a left and then looked back behind him. The man was nowhere in sight. He stopped and retraced his steps for a block, but still didn't see the man.

He couldn't have lost him already, not that easily. Something was wrong. Obviously, the man had *let* him go, but why?

He turned and started running, heading for the hotel, only to stop after half a block. He'd gotten himself turned around.

He wasn't sure which way the hotel was.

Chapter Twenty-Three

Sally Murcer didn't want to get out of bed. It was still warm from Clint's body, and she didn't want to let that warmth go.

Still, she could feel the excitement growing inside her at the prospect of traveling on the train to Chicago. As exciting as going to Chicago was, though, there could be death waiting for her there, or even on the train.

Why had she bothered to wire Washington that she was a witness? Her life would be so much easier now if she had just kept her mouth shut and gone on working at Russell's ranch. Or she could even have quit and moved on. Why did she have to put her life in danger?

Then again, if she *hadn't* wired Washington she would never have met Clint Adams.

She rolled onto her back and continued looking for some good reason to get up.

Conrad reached the hotel and went into the lobby. He decided to play it boldly, maybe unnerve this Adams character, make him make a mistake.

He went to the front desk to bribe a room number out of the clerk.

Chapter Twenty-Four

Clint had finally managed to get himself straightened out, and found his way to the hotel. He hurried up the steps to the second floor, drawing curious looks from people in the lobby and on the stairs themselves. He rushed down the hall to the room he was sharing with Sally and tried the door. It was locked and he pulled his key out and quickly unlocked it.

"Sally!" he shouted.

No answer.

He closed the door behind him and shouted again, louder, "Sally?"

He ran into the bedroom and banged right into her as she was coming out. She was naked, and soaking wet. The water made her skin look shiny. He grabbed her so that he wouldn't knock her over.

"Get dried off."

"But I'm not finished—"

"Yes, you are. Get dried off and get dressed."

He released her and as she dried herself he told her about the man who had followed him.

"But you just said you lost him," she said when he was finished. "Why do we have to leave the hotel if you lost him?"

"I didn't lose him," Clint said, "he let me lose him. He probably came here ahead of me."

"And you were worried about me?" she said. "You thought that he might have come up here after me?"

"That's what I thought," he said, breathlessly. "Thank God I was wrong."

She tried to hide her pleasure at the fact that he'd been so worried—so *scared*—for her.

"What are we going to do?"

"We're going to get dressed and get out of here. We'll have to find someplace else to stay until the train leaves this afternoon."

"You got the tickets?"

"Yes," he said. "I managed to get one of the sleeping quarters."

"You mean like a room on the train?"

"A small compartment."

She was dressed now, wearing one of the simpler dresses they'd bought. Her other things she packed into his saddlebags with his stuff. He was wearing the suit, so all he had were a pair of trousers and an extra shirt. Still the saddlebags bulged. They need something a little less noticeable to carry their gear in.

"How do we get out of the hotel without being seen?" she asked.

"Whoever the man is, he can only watch the front or the back. We'll assume he's watching the front and we'll go out the back."

"When he realizes he *has* lost us, won't he go to the railroad station?"

"You're getting good at this," Clint said. "We'll have to figure a way past him."

"Do you know what he looks like?"

"I think so, but he's bound to have some help, and I won't know them."

"What do we do, then?"

"Well, the first thing we have to do is get rid of that," he said, looking at her.

"Get rid of what?"

"Your red hair."

"Oh no, I am not cutting off my hair!" she said, warningly.

"I didn't say you had to cut it," he said, "we just have to . . . get it out of sight."

"And how do you propose to do that?"

"I don't know," he said. "I'll have to think about it. Are you ready to leave?"

"I'm ready."

Chapter Twenty-Five

They went out into the hall and Clint looked both ways before telling her, "That way."

"That's not the way to the lobby."

"We're not going to the lobby," he said. "We're going to find a back way out."

They walked down the hall until they found a stairway going down.

"Let's see where this leads," he said.

They went down the stairway and Clint knew where it led before they reached the bottom. He could smell food, and hear pots and pans rattling. When they got to the bottom of the stairs they found themselves right outside the kitchen.

"Now what?" she asked.

"Let's go in," he said. "There's got to be a back door."

They entered the kitchen and started to walk through.

"Hey," a big, florid-faced man yelled. He was dressed in white and wearing a chef's hat. "This is the kitchen. No guests are allowed in here."

"We're sorry," Clint said, "but we're looking for a back door."

The man frowned and said, "You lookin' to run out on your bill?"

Clint knew he had to come up with a story that the man would believe. When he saw the way the man was looking at Sally, he thought he had one.

"No, we're not trying to run out on our bill," Clint said. "We're, uh, trying to avoid her husband."

"Husband, huh?" A knowing look came into the man's eyes.

"He's in the lobby," Sally said, catching up quickly. "He had a detective follow us here and I think he wants to *kill* us."

"Kill you, huh?" the man asked, looking Sally up and down. No man in his right mind would want to see a woman like Sally Murcer dead.

"Can you help us?" she asked. "Please?"

The man studied her a few moments longer, then said, "Sure, missy. I sure wouldn't want to see your body get any holes in it."

"Oh, thank you," she said, ignoring the leer he sent her way.

"Follow me."

They followed the man through the kitchen until they reached a back door.

"That way out," he said, pointing to a back exit from the kitchen.

"Bless you," Sally said, and planted a kiss on the man's cheek for good measure. The man looked surprised, and touched his cheek where her lips had been.

She went out the door and as Clint moved past the man to follow her he heard him say, "You lucky dog!"

Clint couldn't resist looking at the man and giving him a big smile.

When they got several blocks from the hotel Clint found a store and bought a suitcase that would fit all their clothes. They went into an alley to move their belongings from the saddlebags to the suitcase, and then discarded the saddlebags.

"This should attract less attention," he said, holding the suitcase in one hand, "especially in the railroad station."

"Speaking of that," she said, "have you figured out how we're going to get through the station yet?"

"No, not yet," he said. "I'm still working on that."

"I'm not worried," she said. "You'll think of something."

He wished he had as much confidence in himself as she seemed to have in him.

Chapter Twenty-Six

They still had several hours before their train left. That gave them several hours to come up with some sort of a plan.

One thing that Clint couldn't risk doing now was going back to the livery near the hotel to get Duke. He was going to *have* to leave the big black gelding behind.

"I have to send a telegram," he said to Sally.

"To who?"

"A friend," he said.

They found an office and he sent a telegram to Talbot Roper, the Denver private detective who was a good friend of his, and asked the man to retrieve his horse and take care of him until Clint could come back for him.

"Will he do it?" Sally asked. "Without asking any questions?"

"He'll do it."

"What time is it?" she asked, as they left the telegraph office.

He checked his watch and said, "It's eleven. We have just under two hours."

"So what's your plan for getting into the station?"

He only half heard her questions. He was looking into the backyard they were standing near, at the laundry that was hanging on a line to dry.

"What is it?" she asked, noticing that his attention was elsewhere.

"Is this place what I think it is?" he asked.

She looked at the brick and stone building behind them and asked, "What is it?"

"I'll be damned," he said. "We're behind the police station."

"Should we go in and ask for help?"

"No," he said. "Wait here."

"Where are you going?" she asked.

"To climb a fence. Keep your eyes open and let me know if anyone is coming."

"Clint—" she started, but he had already started over the low fence into the backyard of the police property.

She watched as he grabbed a few items from a laundry line and then scrambled back over the fence.

"You're stealing those things."

"You're right," he said, giving her the bundle. "Wait here."

He climbed back over and affixed some paper money to the clothespins he had taken the clothes from, then he rejoined her.

"Let's find a hotel."

"What do you have in mind?" she asked.

"We just need someplace to change, honey," he said. "That's all."

Lex Luger and his men had arrived during the night, and had decided that the best thing they could do was position themselves at the train station. They went directly there and split up.

"We might have missed them already," Vinton pointed out.

"We might have," Luger said, "but we'll have to take a chance. We were only a day behind them, and if they didn't catch a train yesterday, then they have to catch one today. They can't risk staying in Denver for too long. Just take up position, and we'll wait."

Frank Conrad recognized Lex Luger as Robert Russell's foreman. He had seen the man once or twice before. He also saw the two men that Luger had brought with him. Conrad decided not to reveal himself to Luger and his men. He was going to stay behind the scenes and maybe he'd be able to pick up some pieces when it was all over.

When the policemen entered the station they drew some nervous glances from Lex Luger and his men. The last thing they needed was the police to be involved.

One of the policemen was tall, the other shorter. The short one was heavyset and out of shape. Still, Luger didn't want to tangle with the law. He'd have to explain that to Russell later on.

He watched as the two policeman walked to the

train and got on. He forgot about them then and continued to watch for Clint Adams and Sally Murcer.

Frank Conrad saw the two policemen and started laughing hard on the inside.

As the train for Chicago pulled out of the station Lex Luger crossed over to his two men and said, "Come on. I've got to find a telegraph office and send a message to the boss. He's not gonna like this."

Luger wondered if he could somehow place the blame on the two men who were with him.

On the train Clint Adams said, "Come on, we have to find our compartment before a porter or the conductor sees us."

"Why?"

"If we're spotted we'll have to wear these things for the whole trip, or someone will get suspicious."

"Which way do we go?"

"Let's try down here."

They moved to the next car and continued up the aisle. As they were entering the car they came face to face with the conductor.

"Officers," the man said, "can I help you?"

Well, Clint thought, we've been seen, so there's no harm in asking.

"Ah, yes, I wonder if you could direct us to the correct car?"

"Certainly," the man said. "Can I see your tickets, please?"

Clint handed them over. The conductor glanced at them and then handed them back.

"Just walk down two cars, Officer," the man said. "You'll find it easy enough. The numbers are right on the doors."

"Thank you."

"Have a pleasant trip, officers. I'll feel a little safer with a couple of officers of the law on board."

"Thank you," Clint said.

Sally purposely kept silent. The rags they had stuffed her uniform with hid her figure, and her hair was tucked up under the hat, but if she spoke it would give away the fact that she was a woman.

"We'd better get to our compartment before we run into somebody else," Clint said.

Frank Conrad hurriedly bought a ticket for the Chicago train and managed to jump onto the train as it was moving out of the station.

Chapter Twenty-Seven

It was better than a thousand miles to Chicago and, with the stops the train would make along the way, the trip would take the better part of three days.

Clint and Sally took their meals in the dining car and found that a lot of respect was afforded policemen. Clint was even able to wear his holster out in the open with no question.

Since the conductor knew them as policemen they decided to wear the clothing whenever they left the compartment.

Clint wondered if the conductor had noticed that they had tickets for the same compartment.

For two days Frank Conrad watched the "policemen," waiting for an opportunity to catch one without the other. Unfortunately, that opportunity never arose, and he decided that he was going to have to take them both at one time if he was going to complete his assignment before the train reached Chicago.

It was late the night of the third day, and the next morning they would be pulling into Chicago.

Sally was insatiable that night. She was excited about being in Chicago, and about the way they were able to move around the train without being "seen."

"Jesus," he said at one point, "can't you get enough?"

"Do you mind?"

"Not if I don't die by morning."

She was sitting astride him, his erection buried deep inside of her, when she said to him, "I'm hungry."

"What?"

"Hungry."

"Me, too," he said, taking her breast in his mouth.

Later she said, "I mean I'm really hungry. Do you think we can get something from the dining car now?"

"Why not?" he asked.

She moved on him then, bouncing up and down quickly, breathing raggedly as she drove both of them to the point of release . . .

They dressed later and as they were walking to the dining car Sally suddenly said, "I don't feel right about this."

"About what?"

"About expecting special treatment because they think we're somebody we're not."

"Do you want to go back to the compartment?" he asked.

She thought it over for a moment, weighing her guilt against her hunger, and then said, "No, let's eat."

Frank Conrad couldn't believe his luck. He had been watching their compartment from the far end of the car. They wouldn't pass him unless they had some reason to go to the stock car. When he saw them step out and start the other way he waited until they went through the door to the next car, and then followed.

He finally tracked them to the dining car, where a black waiter was making a fuss about getting them something to eat.

" . . . whatever you want, Officers," the waiter was saying. "Just name it."

"If you've got some cold chicken," Sally said, deepening her voice, "that would be nice . . ."

"Ah could have some hot chicken made fo' you—" the man offered.

"Cold chicken would be fine," Clint said. Beside him Sally was trying to keep from laughing out loud.

Conrad waited while Adams and the woman ate. He hoped they were enjoying their late night meal.

It was the last meal they would ever have.

Chapter Twenty-Eight

"How was it, Officer?" the black waiter asked.

"It was wonderful," she said. "I would tip you, but—"

"Ah wouldn't take it anyways, Officer," the man said. "Ah'm just glad you enjoyed it."

"Very much," she said.

As they walked back to their compartment Clint said, "You're getting too cocky. Don't speak to anyone else."

"Okay," she said in her deep voice, and then she laughed behind her hands.

They had just stepped back into their car when Clint felt a gun pressed against the small of his back.

"Just stand easy, Officer," the man said, putting extra emphasis on the word "Officer."

"You the fella who was following me all around Denver?" Clint asked.

"That was me. Hand over your gun, nice and easy."

Clint took his gun from his holster and handed it to the man.

"Thank you," the man said as he took the gun. Conrad stuck the gun into his own belt. "Now you and the lady are going for a walk with me."

"How far?"

"Just as far as the stock car. If anyone steps out of their compartment, Adams, don't try anything funny. I'll pull the trigger on the girl first. Understand?"

"Understood."

With his eyes Clint warned Sally against trying anything.

They walked the length of the car, Clint and Sally walking side by side with Conrad right behind them. It had not escaped Clint's notice that the man knew his name. That meant he knew who they both were, which meant he worked for Robert Russell. *That* meant that he couldn't be bought off. Clint just wouldn't have enough money to do the job.

When they reached the end of the car without running into anyone Conrad said to Clint, "Open the door . . . easy."

Clint did so and they stepped between the cars.

"Now into the stock car."

Clint opened that door and they stepped in. They could smell the horses and the horse manure. Conrad closed the door behind them and then gave Clint a push.

"Stand over there with him, miss," Conrad said.

Sally stepped over next to Clint.

"Take that hat off your head, miss."

"Why?" Sally asked.

"He wants to make sure he has the right woman," Clint said. "Go ahead, take it off."

Sally took off the cap and her luxurious red hair fell down around her shoulders.

"You *are* beautiful."

"I suppose I should be flattered."

"If you like. I was just stating a fact. I guess you got that uniform stuffed with rags, huh?"

She didn't answer.

"How do you expect to kill two people on this train and get away with it?" Clint asked.

"No one saw us come in here," Frank Conrad said. "I'll just put your bodies in with the horses. They won't be found until we get to Chicago, and I'll be on the next train back to Denver."

"You've got it all figured out," Clint said.

"I usually do before I make my move."

"You want us to turn our backs and make it easy for you?"

"Nobody said it was going to be easy," Frank Conrad said, growling. "It's just something that has to be done."

"Then go ahead and do it," Sally said, "but shoot me first."

"Don't want to see your man die, huh?"

"Come on, mister," Sally said, "shoot me. See if you're man enough."

"You doubtin' my manhood, lady?" Conrad asked.

"That's right," she said. "I think you've been gelded, friend. You're only half a man."

"I tell you what," Conrad said. "I'll shoot Adams first, and then you and me can see how *gelded* I really am, huh?"

"I doubt it."

"Get undressed," he told her. "Get rid of that uniform and the rags. I want to see your body."

"Sure, friend," she said, "but it won't make a difference."

Abruptly she unbuttoned the shirt she was wearing, and a rolled up dress fell out. She removed the shirt and was naked to the waist. Her breasts had goosebumps all over them, and her nipples were hard.

"My God," Conrad said, staring at her.

Clint was watching the man, waiting for a chance to move, but Sally didn't give him a chance. She stuck her hand into her pants and came out not with the rolled up dress that was in there, but with Clint Adams's Colt New Line. She pointed the little gun at Frank Conrad and fired.

Conrad was shocked to feel the bullet drive into his chest. He looked over at the red-haired woman and saw the gun in her hand . . . and then he saw nothing. . . .

"I'm glad you had me wear the gun on the inside of my pants," Sally said to Clint.

Clint heaved Frank Conrad's body up and then let it fall into the empty stall. Putting him in stall already occupied by a horse might agitate the horse, and they didn't want anything drawing attention to the body until they were long gone from the train.

That done he turned to Sally and said, "So am I. We're lucky he didn't search you."

"Do you think anyone heard the shot?" she asked.

"Let's not wait around to find out," he said. "Get your cap and let's get back to our compartment."

"Who was he?" she asked, pinning her hair back up.

Clint looked at the man's wallet.

"His name was Frank Conrad, and according to this he was a private detective."

"Working for Russell?"

"Undoubtedly."

"I'm ready," Sally said, having successfully donned her disguise again. She tucked her hair back underneath the cap.

"So am I," he said. "Come on."

They left the stock car and hurried back to their compartment, where they both stripped off their disguises and dressed in normal clothes.

They didn't make love that night. There were too many other things on their minds.

Frank Conrad was the first man she had ever killed, and she was amazed that she didn't feel anything. She didn't feel happy or sad, she just felt empty. Curiously, she went through the dead man's wallet.

Clint knew that Conrad was the first man Sally had ever killed just by the way she was leafing through the man's wallet, as if she was trying to find out who he was now that she had killed him.

Clint hoped she wouldn't find any photographs of a wife, or of children, in there.

Chapter Twenty-Nine

The next morning, when the train pulled into Chicago, the body of Frank Conrad had yet to be discovered. Or, as Clint told Sally, perhaps it had, but it was being kept quiet. The owners of the railroad certainly did not want it to be known that their passengers were murdered on their trains.

As they pulled into the station Clint looked out the window and said, "Well, there are no uniformed police in the station."

"What about Robert Russell's men?"

"They could very well be there," Clint said, still looking around.

"Do you think they realized in Denver what we did?"

"If they did, then Russell's men will be looking for two uniformed Denver police."

107

For that reason they were wearing their regular clothes.

"All right, Sally," Clint said, straightening his collar. "Let's go and see Chicago."

Michael John stood in the Chicago train station, looking for a stunning redhead and a tall, dark-haired man. He had been told that, in the event that the man and woman got out of Denver alive, they would be heading for Chicago and would become his responsibility.

John was not a private investigator. He made no excuses about what he did. Sometimes he broke bones, sometimes he broke heads, and sometimes he just flat out killed people, and he did it all for money.

Clint decided that they would walk all the way to the last car and then leave the train.

"Now what?" she asked. "The station is down there."

He looked around. They were in a train yard, and there were other trains scattered about, not in use.

"Come on," he said, "we'll find our way to the street this way. Hopefully, they'll concentrate all their efforts on the station itself."

Robert Russell was having dinner in the D.C. Royale Hotel dining room. His dinner companion was a very attractive brunette in her late thirties. She had long hair, a handsome face, and a stunning figure. According to Phillip Gordon she was not a whore, she was just a woman who enjoyed the company of wealthy men.

Robert Russell certainly fit that description.

Her name was Bonnie Rose, but she told Robert Russell he could call her "Bonnie" or "Rosie." Russell didn't care what he called her as long as she ended up in his bed.

After dinner Russell asked Bonnie if she would like to come upstairs and see his suite. She managed to look demure as she accepted.

When they reached his room he put his hand on her bare shoulders and then slid her gown down until her breasts were exposed. They were large, not as firm as they might have been when she was in her twenties, but they were fine for Robert Russell's purpose. He filled his hands with them, squeezing them so that the nipples popped out between his fingers. He leaned over and licked the nipples and the woman reached for his trousers. In moments she had his pants and underwear down around his legs and was marveling at the size of his swollen penis.

"You have the biggest dick I've ever seen," she said.

Russell took that bit of information with a grain of salt. She knew that how much money she got depended on how good a performance she gave. He knew he had a big penis, but it certainly wasn't the biggest she had ever seen. Still, he didn't mind being lied to.

She leaned forward then, wetting him thoroughly with her tongue before she finally took him in her mouth. Her left hand fondled his testicles, her right encircled whatever portion of his penis was not in her mouth. She rode him up and down, wet, moaning and sucking so that he rose up onto his toes. He reached down to cup her head, but allowed her to dictate the tempo as her mouth continued to glide over him. He felt his orgasm building in his balls, the trembling in his thighs—and then there was a knock on the door. She let his penis pop free, and it glistened with her saliva. The air hit it and it felt incredibly cold and started to shrivel.

"Damn!" he swore. "Would you wait in the bedroom, my dear?"

"Of course, Robert," she said, "but don't be long." She stood and gave him a kiss that stiffened his cock again. The kiss seemed to be all tongue, and then she walked naked into the bedroom.

Russell, cursing inside, pulled up his pants and covered his raging cock. He didn't bother to button them, or to tighten his belt.

He pulled the door open and snapped, "I'm a little busy at the moment, Gordon!" Russell said from between clenched teeth. He was aware that his penis was still pulsating.

Phillip Gordon looked down at his employer's trousers and said, "Oh, yes, of course . . . but I thought this was important enough to—to interrupt you, sir."

Russell sighed heavily and said, "All right, what is the news?"

"Clint Adams and the woman, Sally Murcer," Gordon said, "they made it out of Denver."

"Damn!" Robert Russell said. "Have you heard from Frank Conrad?"

"Not from him," Gordon said, "but I have heard, er, *of* him."

"What the hell does that mean?" Russell demanded.

Gordon took a deep breath and then said, "His body was found in one of the stock cars of the train from Denver to Chicago."

"They killed him," Russell said. "They were on that train and they killed him."

"It would seem so."

"What about Luger?"

"I've heard from him, too," Gordon said. "He and his men were unable to catch up to them. They got as far as the Denver train station."

"And they didn't see Adams and the woman get on the train?" Russell asked, incredulously.

"Apparently only Conrad did."

Russell's jaw worked angrily.

"Who do we have in Chicago?"

"A man named Michael John."

"What does he do?"

"Um, he's a killer."

"Is he any good?" Russell asked, then continued without waiting for an answer. "Never mind. That doesn't matter. He's all we have at the moment. Wire him and tell him that he gets a double bonus if Adams and the woman don't make it out of Chicago."

"And if they do?"

"If they manage to get on the train from Chicago to here," Robert Russell said, "then we'll just have to let Stark do what he does best."

"It won't look good, sir, if they are killed here in Washington."

"It will look even worse if the woman makes it to the witness stand," Russell said. "Send that wire to Chicago . . . and send one firing Luger and whoever the men are who are with him."

"Yes, sir."

"And don't bother me again tonight."

"Yes, sir. I'll see you in the morning."

"Don't make it too early."

"Yes, sir. I mean, no, sir."

Robert Russell slammed the door in Gordon face and then dropped his pants, kicked them away and walked toward the bedroom.

Chapter Thirty

"Excuse me, sir?"

"Yes?" William Masters Cartwright said to the man who had stuck his head in the door of his office. "What is it, Nelson?"

Nelson Coleman entered the room and closed the door behind him, then turned to face his boss. Coleman was a relative newcomer to the Secret Service, having been hired several months earlier as Cartwright's administrative assistant.

"We have some news from Chicago, sir."

"Of Clint Adams?"

"It may be connected, sir."

"Well, what is it?"

"It seems that a man named Frank Conrad was found dead in the stock car of the Denver to Chicago train this morning."

"Conrad?" Cartwright said. "Who was he?"

"A private inquiry agent from Denver."

"A detective?"

"Yes, sir."

"What does that have to do with us?"

"Well, sir," Nelson Coleman said with his customary dramatic flair, "we've found that he's had some dealings with Robert Russell in the past."

Cartwright slapped the arm of the chair he was seated in and said softly, "They're alive."

"It could very well mean that, sir."

Cartwright ignored the man's comment.

"Nelson, I want a railroad schedule for the next three trains out of Chicago," he said. "We're going to have men at the station waiting for them when they get off."

"Yes, sir," Coleman said, "I'll get those for you right away."

As Cartwright's assistant left, the head of the Secret Service gripped the arms of his chair tightly. This was the first indication they'd had for some time that Adams might be alive. Maybe the man was actually going to make it—and with the girl.

On his way to the train station to pick up the schedules for his boss, Nelson Coleman made a stop at the D.C. Royale Hotel.

Chapter Thirty-One

The hotel Clint picked in Chicago was small and rundown, just off of Michigan Avenue. The clerk had smirked at them when Clint checked them in, and there was a drunk sleeping on the steps that they had to step over on the way up.

The room itself actually wasn't that bad. It was about the same as some of the rooms Clint had stayed in before in some smaller towns.

Sally made a comment much to that effect.

"I feel like I'm back in Wells," she said. "This is like the first room I had when I arrived there."

"The view's a little different," he said, looking out the window.

The sidewalks were paved and the streets were cobblestone, and some of the building here made the buildings in Denver seem small.

"Did you notice how many people were on the streets as we walked here?" Sally said to him later that evening.

"I did."

"I think I'll testify and then get right back on the train and head west again."

Sally was losing her awe of the big cities very quickly.

They had eaten dinner at a small cafe near the hotel where the food was greasy and the coffee weak.

"When does our train leave?" she asked when they got back to the room.

He checked the schedule and said, "Two tomorrow afternoon. I'm sorry, but we'll have to stay here until then."

"I know," she said. She moved on the bed and the springs squeaked. The mattress was so thin they might as well not have had one.

He sat next to her and took her hand.

"I know this has been rough on you, Sally, but you've really stood up to it all."

"Have I?"

"Hell, you saved my life on that train," he said, reminding her.

"I also saved my life."

"You saved both our lives through quick thinking."

"It was your idea for me to carry that little gun inside my trousers."

"But it was you who had the presence of mind to take it out and pull the trigger."

"I know," she said to him, her eyes filling with tears. "I was so scared," she said, her voice barely audible.

"I know," he said, taking her in his arms so she could cry it out.

On the train he had taken Frank Conrad's wallet away from her, and as they walked out of the station he had dumped into a trash receptacle.

He held her until she had cried so much that she became sleepy. They lay down on the bed side by side, fully dressed.

While she slept next to him Clint lay awake and wondered what would be waiting for them at the Chicago train station tomorrow—or at the Washington station when they arrived there.

His decision not to contact Cartwright had been made after much thought. Robert Russell was so wealthy that he could very well have someone working for him who was on the government payroll, as well. Cartwright was the only man Clint would trust with Sally, and he had no intention of turning her over to anyone but him.

His original intention had been to deliver the woman to Cartwright in Washington and then head back west. Now he had decided to stay and make sure that she lived through the trial and got started back west herself.

He knew that Sally was becoming serious about him, and he was sorry about that. He didn't want to hurt her, but as much as he liked her—*more* than just liked her—he didn't see himself spending the rest of his life with her, or with any woman.

He hoped that when the time came to go their separate ways, she'd understand that.

Knowing what he did about her, he thought she would, and he felt sure she'd handle it.

If she could handle everything that had happened to them since leaving Wells, Arizona, she could handle anything.

Michael John had people out combing the streets of Chicago for Adams and the woman, Sally Murcer. The only thing one of them had come up with was some discarded Denver police uniforms on the train. That was obviously how they had gotten out of Denver, but they hadn't gotten past him that way.

John sat in a small, greasy restaurant that was his headquarters, waiting for word from one of his people that they had spotted the woman. It was the woman he had everyone out looking for, because her red hair would make her easy to spot. Unless she and the man had disguised themselves once again.

John knew the train schedules by heart. He knew there was a train leaving for Washington at two P.M., and then not another one until nine P.M. He felt sure that Adams would try to get the girl on the two P.M. train. He'd have men in the station all day, though, just to be sure.

Over his dinner John thought about how he would kill them. He'd killed women before, most of them whores, so it didn't bother him that he was going to kill a woman. If she was as lovely as Gordon had indicated in his wire, it would be a damned waste, but he'd do it. With the money he was going to make he could buy himself five lovely women. Maybe they'd be whores, but he'd known some pretty beautiful whores in his time.

Hell, he'd *killed* some pretty beautiful whores.

Chapter Thirty-Two

Clint woke Sally early the next morning to tell her that he was going to the train station to pick up the tickets.

"Well, I'm going with you," she said.

"No," he said, firmly, "you're not. You're going downstairs to that greasy cafe we found and have breakfast. Eat slow and wait for me there."

"They could be waiting for you at the station," she argued. "You could need my help."

"Sally," he said, "you're the one they're looking for, not me. You know that. I'll have a better chance of going unnoticed without you."

"I'll pad myself again and cover my hair," she said. "I'm going with you. You need someone to cover your back."

"Sally—"

"I did pretty well on the train, didn't I?" she reminded him.

He paused and then was forced to admit, "Yes, you did, you did fine on the train."

"So?"

"So," he said, feeling defeated, "let's go have breakfast and talk about it."

She pinned her hair up, put on her hat, and they left the room. Anyone looking close enough would be able to see the strands of red hair that peeked out from beneath that hat, but from a distance it was an effective enough disguise.

They left the hotel together and crossed the street to the cafe.

Michael John was just getting ready to pay his check and leave when a man and a woman walked into the cafe. John was unhappy with the results he was getting out of his men. No one in the city had seen a woman with red hair who fit Sally Murcer's description. He figured he was just going to have to go down to the railroad station and wait for them to show up.

The man and woman were being seated as he went out the front door.

Over breakfast Clint continued to try and talk Sally out of going to the station with him.

"I can't help it, Clint," she said. "I'll go mad if I just have to sit and wait."

"Sally, I'm supposed to be keeping you *out* of danger—" he started, but she cut him off.

"This whole *trip* has been dangerous," she said,

"for you as well as me. I don't want to wonder what happened to you if you don't come back, Clint. If you get killed, at least I'll be there."

"I'm not going to get killed—"

"No," she said, "you're not—and there's even less chance of it if I'm there to back you up."

"Sally—"

"Could you please stop trying to talk me out of it?" she asked. "As far as I'm concerned it's settled. I'm going with you.

"All right, all right," he said. "I swear, I've never known a more stubborn woman—you're staying outside the station while I go in, do you understand?"

"Sure, I understand," she said, smiling. "You're the boss."

"Now you tell me . . ."

They went back to the hotel and prepared for the walk to the station. Clint left his holster behind. Instead he took his Colt and pushed it down into his belt at the small of his back, then put on the jacket from the new suit he'd bought to cover it.

Next they tore open the pillow on the bed and removed some of the feathers from it. They took the remaining bulky pillowcase, opened Sally's shirt and molded it to her belly, tucked the New Line inside, and closed the shirt.

She looked like a woman who badly needed a diet. The look of her sloppy belly even took away from the thrust of her breasts.

"Well," he said, looking at her critically, "there's not much we can do about your face. Men are still going to look at that, and with your hair up like that they can still see your lovely neck—"

"Stop with the compliments," she said. "I'm still going."

"All right," he said, "all I'm saying is that we've done what we can to disguise you."

"And nothing to disguise you."

"They're not looking for me," he said. "They see men like me on the streets everyday. A woman like you comes along once in a . . ."

"Can we stop with the compliments?" she said. "Isn't it time we got moving?"

"Before we do let's get some things straight."

"Like what?"

"When we get to the station you stay behind me," he said. "You watch me go into the station and to the ticket window. Don't do anything at all that will bring attention to yourself."

"Unless you get into trouble," she said. "If you do, I'm gonna help you."

"If I get into trouble, Sally," Clint said, slowly, "the best thing for you to do would be to run right back here."

"That's not why I'm going," she said. "If I was just going to be thinking of myself, Clint, I'd just stay right here."

"Well, that sounds like a good—"

"Don't start that again," she said. "I'm going. We settled that."

"All right," he said, shaking his head, "but if you get killed because you won't listen to me I'll never forgive you."

"If I get killed," she said, "I promise never to bother you again."

He grabbed her and hugged her to him.

"Neither one of us is getting killed, Sally," he said, "neither one of us."

Chapter Thirty-Three

During the walk to the station Sally walked about half a block ahead of Clint. He didn't want it to look as if they were together, but he wanted to be able to keep an eye on her. He was also able to watch their backtrail, just in case they had already been spotted and were being followed. As far as he could tell, they hadn't, and they weren't.

When they reached the station she stopped and stood off to one side while he went in, keeping a sharp eye out. It was early, but there were plenty of people there, buying tickets, waiting for trains to arrive or depart. It would have been very easy for Russell's men to hide among the crowd. At least he didn't see any uniformed police. He hadn't read anything in the newspaper about the body of Frank Conrad being found. He wondered if Cartwright had anything to do with that. If Cartwright had heard about the body,

and the man had a history of working for Robert
Russell, then Cartwright was probably figuring that
Clint and the woman were alive.

Maybe in killing Conrad, they had effectively left
Cartwright a message that they were alive.

Cautiously Clint approached the ticket window and
waited behind a man and a woman. He risked a
glance behind him and saw Sally, who looked for
all the world like a dumpy woman either waiting
for a train or waiting for her man to come in on a
train.

Standing behind the man, who was asking for a
ticket on the same train that he wanted, Clint noticed
another man standing off to the side, within earshot.
When the man received his ticket and walked away,
the man standing nearby also walked away. Clint
took a moment to confirm that one man was following
the other. When he looked back to where the second
man had been standing, within easy earshot of the
window, there was another man standing there, trying to look nonchalant.

Clint felt sure that Robert Russell had men watching the station, following anyone who bought a ticket
for a train to Washington. He quickly studied the
schedule again. There was a two P.M. train to
Washington, and a nine P.M. train. Maybe they
were watching for people buying tickets on the
two P.M.

As Clint stepped up to the window he put the schedule on the counter, upside down so the clerk could see
it, and pointed to that train.

"Whatsamatta?" the clerk asked. "Can't talk?"

Clint leaned into the window and said, "I just don't

want everybody knowing my business. I need two tickets, please."

The man swallowed, looked down at the schedule, pointed to the nine P.M. train and asked, "For that one?"

"Yes, for that one."

The man handed the tickets over and accepted payment.

"Thank you," Clint said, and walked away. It took a concerted effort not to look behind him.

As he passed Sally in front of the station he said quickly, "See if I'm being followed."

She gave him a slight nod of understanding and he went on.

He walked a couple of blocks and then stopped to wait for Sally. She appeared several moments later.

"Did you see a man standing near the ticket window?" he asked.

"Yes."

"Did he follow me?"

"No."

"Are you sure?"

"Positive."

"Well, maybe my theory was right."

"What theory?"

"That they'd be looking for people buying tickets on the two o'clock train."

"What did you buy?"

"Tickets on the nine P.M."

"So now we're taking the nine o'clock train?"

"No," he said, "we're still getting on the two o'clock train."

"With the wrong tickets?"

"So we'll pretend we got on the wrong train. They're not going to put us off."

"So what do we do in the meantime?"

"Well, since we're not being followed," he said, "maybe we'll do some following of our own."

Chapter Thirty-Four

"You what?" Michael John asked.

"I was only following guys who bought tickets on the two P.M. train," Jeff John said to his cousin. "I mean, they'd want to get tickets on the first train, wouldn't they?"

"Jeffrey," Michael John said. "Don't you think they would know that?"

"Huh?"

Jeffrey John was Michael John's cousin, his cross to bear in the world. Since Jeff was the only family John had, he tried to look out for him. Jeff was younger, weaker, and Lord, was he dumber!

Michael John had stopped by the station to check in with the people he had following anyone who bought a ticket on a train to Washington. According to Jeff, a man bought a ticket on the nine P.M., just moments before John had arrived, and Jeff hadn't bothered following him.

"Don't you think, Jeff?"

"Huh? Sure, I think. I just thought—"

"Well, don't think," Michael said, cutting his cousin off. "Just do like I tell you, all right?"

"Come on, Michael," Jeff said, "he bought a ticket on the nine o'clock train, not the two o'clock train."

"Idiot!" John said. "I wanted anyone followed who bought a ticket on either train."

"Yeah, but, wouldn't it make sense for them to want to leave on the earlier—"

"Jeff!" John snapped.

"What, Mike?"

"Shut up! Don't think, Jeff, just don't think. The next person who buys a ticket on either train to Washington, you follow him. If he meets with a red-haired woman, you come back and tell me. Okay?"

"Mike—"

"Do you understand, Jeff?"

"Sure, Mike, sure," Jeffrey John said, his tone wounded, "I understand."

Jeff went back to stand near the ticket window, and Michael went and sat on a bench to watch him.

He wanted to make sure that *this* time the dumb fuck did what he was told!

"That's him," Clint said to Sally. "He's following someone else."

They were standing outside the train station, in the doorway of a closed store, waiting for that same man to come out, tailing someone.

"See him?" he asked.

"I see him."

"I'm going to follow him, Sally," he said. "You go back to the hotel."

"Clint—"

"If we both try to follow him," Clint explained, "he's going to notice it."

"What are you going to do?"

"I'll tell you when I get back to the hotel," he said. "I've got to go now or risk losing him. Get back to the hotel and wait for me!"

Clint stepped out of the doorway and started down the street, following the man who was following a man who had bought a ticket on a train going from Chicago to Washington, D.C.

Sally stayed in the doorway for a few moments, struggling with her conscience. She knew Clint was right. Two people could not safely follow another and go unnoticed.

Finally, she stepped out of the doorway and started the other way, back to the hotel. She didn't see the man stepping out of the station.

Michael John stepped out of the station, satisfied that his cousin was finally doing the right thing. He was about to go back in when he noticed the woman.

He didn't know why she caught his eye, but she did. He watched her as she walked down the street. She appeared to be carrying too much weight in her belly—sloppy weight—but she looked familiar to him. Michael John had excellent eyesight and from where he was he could see that her face was beautiful. It was a pity that a woman as good-looking as that didn't take better care of herself . . . and then it hit him.

She was the woman he saw in the cafe that morning. She looked different now—about twenty pounds different—but that was easily accounted for. What if she *wanted* to look twenty pounds heavier? The question then would be *why?*

Because she didn't want to be recognized.

He decided to follow her and try to get a better, closer look at her.

If she had red hair under that hat, he might have just hit the jackpot.

Chapter Thirty-Five

Clint followed the man from the station, being careful to keep track of the turns they were taking. He had to get back to the station because he knew how to get back to the hotel from there. He didn't want the same situation that happened in Denver. He couldn't afford to get lost in Chicago.

He'd followed the man for about ten blocks and then quickened his pace, and when he was right behind the man Clint grabbed his elbow.

"Hey!" the man said, turning around. "What the hell's goin' on—"

Clint had moved his gun from the small of his back to the front of his belt. Now he moved his jacket to show the man the gun.

"It wouldn't take me long to kill you, fella," Clint said.

"There's too many people," the other man said, nervously.

"You want to take the chance I can't kill you and melt into the crowd that'll form around your body?"

"What do you want?" the man asked, sullenly.

"I want to talk."

"About what?"

"Let's get off the street," Clint said. In spite of what he had told the man he did not want to have to produce his gun on a crowded Chicago street.

"Mister—"

"I'm the man you're looking for," Clint said.

"What?"

"You heard me."

"You?" the man said. "You're the one with the red-haired woman?"

"That's right."

"Well, I'll be—" the man said. "Michael sure is gonna be happy when I tell him I caught you."

The man looked so pleased with himself that Clint almost hated to break the news to him that *he* was the one who had been caught.

Michael John followed the woman to the hotel that was right across the street from the greasy cafe he used as his office.

"I'll be damned," he said as she entered the hotel. Right across the street from him the whole time.

The thing to do now was go across the street, find her room, and kill her . . . but that would mean that Clint Adams would get away. Did they want the woman bad enough to let the man get away?

There was a telegraph office four blocks away, and he decided to go there first, and send a message to Washington, D.C.

Clint chose a small restaurant and offered to buy the man a drink.

When they were settled at a table with a beer each the man said, "My name's Jeff. Michael's my cousin."

"Michael who?"

"You don't know Michael?"

"No, I don't"

"Then why is he after you and the woman?"

"He's working for someone else."

"Oh."

Clint waited a few moments, then said again, "Michael who?"

"Oh, John, Michael John. My name's Jeffrey John. We're cousins. Our fathers were brothers—"

"That's okay," Clint said, "I don't need an explanation of the family tree."

"Oh, we don't have no trees—" the man said.

"I know how it works," Clint said, cutting him off. "Families, I mean."

"Oh, sorry." Jeff sipped his beer and said, "What do we do now?"

Clint was beginning to have his doubts about the man's usefulness. He was obviously too simple to really know anything of his cousin's plans.

"How much do you know about how your cousin plans to cover the station today?"

"What station?"

Clint took refuge in his beer, and then tried again.

"Let's try something simple, Jeff."

"All right," Jeff said, good naturedly.

"Where is Michael now?"

"I don't know where he is."

"Jeff—"

"I know where he *was*."

"All right," Clint said, speaking very slowly, "where was he?"

"When I left the station he was right there."

"In the station?"

"Yep," Jeff said, "right there."

Clint's mind raced. If John was at the station to make sure Jeff did the right thing, had he seen Adams follow Jeff? And if he had, where was he now? Waiting outside?

And then another thought occurred to him.

If John was at the station, he might have seen Sally. Now, there was no reason to believe that he would have recognized her, because there was no reason to believe that he had ever seen her before—unless Russell was circulating a photograph of her.

"Has your cousin ever seen the red-haired woman?"

"Not that I know of."

"Where would you meet your cousin after you followed this man?"

"At a cafe he uses as his office," Jeff said.

"And where is that?"

"Just off of Michigan Avenue, across the street from a hotel called the St. Germaine."

"A run down, greasy-looking cafe with bad food?" Clint asked anxiously.

"That's the one."

Clint was up and moving out the door quickly. Jeff followed him out and shouted, "What am I supposed to tell Michael?"

Clint didn't answer.

Chapter Thirty-Six

When Phillip Gordon read the telegraph message from Chicago he shooed his secretary out of his office. She left, closing the door behind her, and Gordon read the message again. Adams and the girl had been located, but had been split up. Which one was priority? Michael John wanted to know.

Jesus, Gordon thought, running his hand over his face. If he approached Russell with this question the man would hit the ceiling.

Gordon put on his jacket and left his office in a hurry, heading for the nearest telegraph office.

Robert Russell woke that morning feeling pleasantly fatigued. The woman, Bonnie, had turned out to be quite something. She was apparently unable to be sexually satisfied, and so was able to keep up with Robert Russell's own powerful sex drive. In the end, it was he who called an end to the session, suggesting that they get some sleep.

He awoke with the woman next to him. The sheet was thrown carelessly over her, so that her big butt was bare. He recalled taking her from behind, slamming into that fine, padded rear over and over again until he bellowed like a bull and exploded into her. She had moaned and cried and shouted, and although she was a whore—or as good as a whore—he was sure that her responses were real. Though a small man in height, Russell knew that sexually he was as big as any man—and bigger than most. Women, he knew, liked him, and he certainly liked them—especially big women like this one.

He was about to slap that delectable rear to awaken her when there was a knock on the door.

Angrily, he rose, grabbed his robe, wrapped it around himself, and went to answer the door.

"What the hell—" he roared at Phillip Gordon.

"John has found them."

His anger forgotten, Russell said, "Where?"

"In Chicago."

"I *know* that, you fool. Where?"

"A hotel called the St. Germaine."

"Are they dead?"

Gordon hesitated, then said, "Not yet. They've, uh, separated."

"Well, which one has he located?"

"The woman."

"Then she's dead."

"Uh, not yet."

"Gordon—"

"She will be, though," Gordon said. "Very shortly."

"She'd better be," Russell said, "because if she isn't, that moron will be. Make that clear to him, Gordon!" Russell grabbed the little attorney's lapels. "She has to be dead!"

Gordon pulled free of Russell's grasp and said, "I'll do that, sir."

Clint reached the hotel and slowed down across the street from it. He checked the cafe, and then checked the street, but there was no one loitering around. Quickly, he entered the hotel and went up to the room.

As he let himself in she said, "What happened?"

"We have to get out of here," Clint said. "You may have been followed here."

"But . . . how?"

"I'll explain later," he said, gathering their things together. "We have to get out of here . . .now!"

"Will I need my disguise?"

"There's no time," he said. "All we need is to get out of here—now!"

Chapter Thirty-Seven

Clint practically dragged Sally across the street to the cafe, which was empty of customers.

"We're not going to eat, are we?" she asked.

"No."

"I didn't think so."

Inside he left her at a table and asked the waiter who had served them, "Do you know what a man named Michael John looks like?"

The waiter gave him a bored look and said, "Who wants to know?"

Clint grabbed ahold of the man's shirt and said, "I do."

The waiter stopped looking bored.

"S-sure, I know him."

"I want you to point him out to me."

"H-he ain't here!"

"I know that," Clint said. He pushed the man toward

the front window and joined him there. "Just keep looking out this window, and when you see him, you point him out to me."

"Mister," the waiter said, "th-this could get me killed."

Clint took out his gun and said, "That could happen anyway, friend."

"Move away from that window, friend," the waiter said. "I'm watchin'."

For probably the first time in his life Jeffrey John made a correct decision. He decided to go and find his cousin, Michael, and tell him what happened right away.

He was headed to the cafe when he saw Michael across the street, about to enter the St. Germaine Hotel.

"Hey, Michael . . ."

"Across the street by the hotel."

Clint looked across the street and saw a tall, fit-looking man about to enter the hotel.

"That's him?" Clint asked. "Michael John?"

"That's him," the waiter said.

"The man with him," Clint said to Sally, "that's his cousin, the one I followed."

"What are they doing?" she asked.

"Right now," he said, "they think they're going into the hotel to kill us."

"You told him about me?" Michael John asked his cousin.

"He had a gun, Michael."

"Jeff," John said, "do *you* have a gun?"

"Sure I do."

"Did it ever occur to you to use it on him?"

Jeff frowned, and then said, "Gee, maybe I shoulda, huh?"

"Maybe," John said.

"Gee, Michael, I'm sorry—"

Michael John put his hand on his cousin's chest and said, "Forget it, Jeff. I'm going upstairs to take care of the woman."

"Whataya want me to do?"

"Get to the railroad station and come back with some men," Michael John said. "We might be able to catch Adams between here and the station."

"What if he's upstairs with the girl?"

"Then I'll collect a bonus," Michael John said. "Just do as I say, Jeff. Go!"

Clint and Sally watched as one cousin entered the hotel and the other ran off down the street in the direction of the railroad station.

"Where?"

"I don't know," Clint said, "but we've got to stay away from the station for now. We'll just have to find a place to hide out for a while."

Michael John drew his gun, a short-barrelled .32, as he approached the entrance to the hotel room. A dollar had gotten him the room number from the clerk.

He put his back to the wall across from the door, then lifted his foot and kicked out. The door slammed open and he just about leaped into the room, his gun held out in front of him. He saw nothing but an empty room.

He took the time to check the entire suite, but he knew they were gone. The place just *felt* empty.

"Damn it," he swore. "They're headed for the station."

He turned and ran out of the room.

"Wait, wait," Clint said, stopping abruptly.

"What is it?" Sally asked.

"We're running toward the train station."

"We have a train to catch, remember?" Sally asked.

"I know that," he said, "but it's not for a couple of hours yet. Meanwhile, we'll be playing tag between here and there with Michael John and his men. We have to go the other way and find a place to hole up."

"The other way," she said.

"That's right."

"Away from the station?"

"Right."

"Then how do we get *to* the station?"

"I don't know," he admitted, "I haven't figured that out yet. As soon as we find a place to hide, I can work on that."

"So the station is that way," she said, pointing.

"Right."

"And we're going that way," she said, pointing the other way.

"Right again."

"Then we'd better get going," she said. "We'll need all the time we can find to come up with a plan."

• • •

When Michael John came running out of the hotel he saw his cousin Jeff running toward him with three men in tow.

"Is this all you got?" he asked.

One of the other men spoke instead of Jeff.

"We've got some men covering the area between here and the station, boss. I figured that's what you'd want."

"Good work, Kirby," Michael John said. "All right, you three check out the hotel. They're not in their room, but that doesn't mean they're not still in the hotel somewhere."

"Right, boss."

"What do you want me to do, Michael?" Jeff asked as Kirby led the other two men into the hotel.

"Jeff," Michael said, "just stay with me, all right? Don't talk, just follow."

"I can do that," Jeff said.

Chapter Thirty-Eight

"We've got to split up," Clint said.

"What?" Sally's surprise was obvious.

They had found a building with an enclosed stairway to the cellar, and they were sitting in that stairwell.

"We have to separate."

"If *I* suggested that you'd say no," she said. Her tone was accusatory.

"Well, I just thought of a good enough reason to do it."

"What?"

"They won't expect it."

"I don't see why they should," she said. "*I* didn't expect you to suggest it. Tell me, oh master, *why* should we separate?"

"*Because* they won't expect it," he said. "They know that I have to protect you, and that the best way for me to do that is to stay with you."

"So we separate."

"Right."

"And so what? Walk right into the station separately? You think they won't recognize us?"

"They'll recognize you no matter what," he said, "unless we can find some way to change your hair color in the next hour."

"Which we can't."

"Right," he said, "so *I'll* walk into the station alone, but we'll get you an escort."

"What kind of escort?" she asked.

"The best kind," he said, "a *police* escort."

Michael Joseph had the area between the hotel and the train station totally covered, and yet no one had seen any sign of Adams or the girl. That could only mean that Adams had decided to take refuge somewhere *away* from the station. He was smart, but was he smart enough to figure out a way to get *into* the station to catch that two P.M. train?

Only time would tell.

"What do you think?" Clint asked. He had just outlined his idea to Sally.

"It's risky," she said.

"If it works you'll be with a policeman."

"No," she said, "I mean it's risky for *you*."

"I'll be fine," he said. "We both will."

"*If* it works."

"That's right," he said, "if it works—and that's going to depend on you."

"Me?"

He nodded.

"And on how good an actress you are."

"I guess we're about to find out, aren't we?" she asked.

"As soon as we find the nearest police station."

Police Officer Andrew Raglin was on desk duty that night. He *hated* desk duty, but when he saw the red-haired woman enter the station he was *glad* he was on desk duty.

Raglin was in his early forties and unmarried. He enjoyed women much too much to ever tie himself down to one, but if he ever *did* marry, it would be to a woman who would see him the way he wanted to be seen—as a hero.

"Can I help you, young lady?"

"I hope so," Sally said. "I have a problem."

"That's why the police are here, ma'am," Raglin said, "to help the public with their problems."

"Well, mine is sort of . . . personal." She looked down demurely, then raised her eyes to see if the man was buying her act—and he definitely was.

"Well, maybe if you tell me what the problem is I can help you."

"I'm leaving Chicago for good," she said.

"Well," the officer said gallantly, "that sounds like *our* problem, ma'am, not yours."

"You're very nice," she said, "but I have this boy-friend—*ex*-boyfriend—who doesn't want me to leave. He says he'll *kill* me before he lets me leave."

"Is that so?"

"Oh, Officer," she said, "I just *have* to catch the two o'clock train, and I'm so afraid he'll be there waiting for me. I'm afraid of what he will do to me."

Raglin puffed out his chest and said, "Well, we'll just see to it that he doesn't do *anything* to you."

"How will you do that?"

"Well, ma'am," he said, "I could send a policeman to the station with you, but since I am due for a break right about now, why don't I just walk you over there myself?"

"You would do that for me?" she asked.

"Of course I would, miss," he said. "That's my job."

Sally couldn't believe it. She'd found a man who wanted to be somebody's hero—*her* hero!

Chapter Thirty-Nine

Michael John had all of his men at the train station. It was one forty-five, and the train to Washington would be leaving in fifteen minutes. If Adams and the woman didn't show they'd have to try for the nine P.M. train.

At that moment the front doors of the station opened and a women stepped through. She was tall, full-bodied, and had flaming red hair.

"That's got to be her," Michael Joseph said, his voice barely a whisper, but his cousin Jeff heard him and took a look.

"It's her," Jeff said, loudly. "Come on."

"Take it easy," Michael said. "I don't see Adams."

"That'll make her easier to take," Jeff argued.

"Just sit tight," Michael said, and as he did a man stepped through the doors behind the girl.

"A policeman!" Jeff said.

"I can see him," Michael said, annoyed. He remembered the Denver police uniforms that had been found on the train, but this man didn't look like Clint Adams dressed like a policeman. This was a *real* Chicago policeman.

He looked around the station, catching the eye of each of his men and shaking them off.

"Aren't we gonna get her?" Jeff asked.

"Not while she's with a policeman, Jeff," Michael said. "I've got to live in this city, and I can't do that if I kill a policeman."

They watched as the woman and the policeman started across the station floor toward the train. At one point they both looked over to where Michael Joseph was standing and the policeman gave him a look that said: "I dare you."

"What's goin' on?" Jeff asked.

"She got herself a police escort," Michael said, "that's what's going on."

The station doors opened again and a man stepped through, carrying a suitcase. The woman and the uniformed policeman had not yet reached the platform.

"That's him," Jeff said. "That's Clint Adams."

"I figured."

"Ain't we gonna take him?"

"It would be interesting to try," Michael said, "but no."

"Why not?"

Michael looked at Jeff and explained very patiently.

"The policeman is still in the station, Jeff. I don't want to have anything to do with *him*. Besides, once the girl is on the train, Adams is worth nothing to us.

It's *her* they want dead, her alone, or her with him, but nothing was said about him alone."

"Then," Jeff said, "we ain't gonna get paid, are we?"

"No," Michael said, "I guess we aren't."

"Shit," Jeff said.

Michael looked at his cousin in surprise and said, "I couldn't have put it better myself, cousin."

Jeff looked at his cousin and then smiled at the compliment.

"There you go, miss," Officer Raglin said. "There's your train, and not a bit of trouble from your old boyfriend."

"Oh, Officer, I don't know how to thank you," she said, and then she kissed his cheek.

"Well . . ." the man said, his face reddening, "well, that was a right nice way to do it, ma'am."

Clint caught up to them at that point and approached the train with Sally.

"How is it going?" Sally asked in a low voice.

"We'll know once we're on the train," he said.

He helped her up onto the train—like any gentleman would have done—and then climbed aboard himself.

Clint had assumed all along that Michael John would want no part of killing a Chicago policeman. No matter how much Robert Russell was paying him, it would do him no good in the gallows.

As the train started to move Sally grabbed Clint's arm and squeezed it tightly.

"I don't believe it," she said. "We made it."

"Thanks to you," he said. "You're a born actress."

"It was your idea."

"But you pulled it off," he said. "That kiss at the end was sheer genius."

"Yes," she said, smiling, "it was, wasn't it?"

Chapter Forty

When Robert Russell heard from Phillip Gordon that Clint Adams and Sally Murcer had successfully boarded the train to Washington he was beyond anger.

It was time to put this matter entirely into the hands of a professional.

"Notify Stark," he said. "I want to see him now."

William Masters Cartwright was an unhappy man. He had expected Clint Adams to be in Washington already with Sally Murcer. As it stood now they were going to have to get a postponement from the federal court, and it would be the second one. He doubted they'd be able to get a third.

If Adams didn't arrive soon, they'd lose Robert Russell for good.

* * *

No matter how Phillip Gordon looked at it, he was in trouble. If Sally Murcer testified, he was in trouble, either with the law *or* with Robert Russell. The government, once they had convicted Robert Russell, would certainly begin to look into his holdings in earnest. If they did that, they would soon find out Gordon's part in all of it.

And even from prison Robert Russell—who was sure to blame *him* for all of this—would still be able to reach him.

He sincerely hoped that Del Stark would be able to keep any of that from happening.

On the train Clint managed to convince a conductor that they had simply made a mistake in boarding the two P.M. train with nine P.M. tickets.

"My wife bought the tickets," he told the man, "and told me they were for the two P.M. train. I mean, I *told* her to buy tickets for the two P.M. train. Maybe it wasn't even her fault. Maybe the ticket seller just gave her the wrong tickets. Then again, maybe it *is* her fault. You know women, especially the pretty ones. They're not all that smart, you know. I mean—"

"Mister, look," the conductor said, interrupting him, "it's okay with me. I mean, the tickets cost the same, right? Don't worry about it. I just won't be able to give you the compartment you were supposed to have on the nine P.M. I'm sure I can find an empty one, though. I mean, we wouldn't want that pretty wife of yours to have to sleep sitting up, would we?"

"No," Clint said, "we wouldn't."

• • •

"The conductor was so smitten with you that he made sure we got a compartment," Clint said to Sally. "I wouldn't be surprised if he had evicted someone."

Sally sat down, feeling drained. Clint sat next to her and put his arm around her.

"Are you all right?"

"Yes," she said, "I just don't know how to feel."

"How about safe?"

"How safe?" she asked. "What happens when we get to Washington? How safe will I be then?"

"We'll have to worry about that when we get there," he said. "Right now you should get some rest."

"And then something to eat?"

"Of course," he said, "you know I'll feed you. In fact, I'm sure the conductor will make room for us in the dining car. All you'll have to do is smile at him."

"That's one of the easier requests I've had in a while," she said. "What about those men from Chicago, Clint?" she asked. "Do you think any of them got on the train?"

"No," he said, "I think once we got past them they accepted the fact that their part in this was over. It's up to . . ."

"It's up to the men in Washington to kill us, right?" she asked.

He tightened his arm around her and she lay her head on his shoulder.

"Washington's the last stop, Sally," he said. "One way or another, it will all be over soon."

"Which one should I worry about?" she asked. "The one way, or the other?"

•   •   •

Del Stark was tired of sitting around his hotel, doing nothing but bedding whores. It was time for him to do what he did best—kill.

Actually, what he *really* did best was kill, and then get paid for it, and he was going to get paid a *lot* for this one.

Chapter Forty-One

Del Stark knew there was no way he could kill Adams and the girl in the train station. There was bound to be some government men waiting for them there. He was simply at the station to spot them, and then to follow them. Once he knew where the government was keeping them, it would be a simple thing to get to them and kill them. It was very difficult to protect people from being killed, because no matter how many men you put around them, there was always that moment when you *couldn't* protect them, that one moment that men like Del Stark's livelihood depended upon.

Stark prided himself on always being at the right place when that moment arrived.

Cartwright assigned six men to cover the station. His original intention was to assign one of them to oversee the others, but in the end he decided to go to the train station himself and oversee the operation.

He wanted to be right there to put Sally Murcer under protective custody.

Clint was looking out a window as the train pulled into the station.

"There are a lot of people out there," Sally said. "How do we know who are the good guys and who are the bad guys?"

"We don't," he said. "We'd have to let them get close enough to speak to us for that, and I'm not about to do that."

As the train came to a halt he said, "Look around. See the men standing around with their hands in their pockets? Craning their necks? They're looking for us."

"Whose men are they?"

"We can't be sure," Clint said, moving away from the window, "but we have to assume the worst."

He began to gather their belongings, and then decided to hell with them. They could move faster without dragging the suitcase with them, and he said so.

"But . . . my beautiful new dresses . . ." Sally said.

"We'll buy you some new ones," he said, "even more beautiful—but first I want to make sure you'll be alive to wear them."

He picked up the .32 Colt New Line and handed it to her. As she tucked it into the front of her belt, inside her shirt, he strapped on his own gun.

"All right," he said, "let's go."

"Where?"

"First I want to get a better look at the station, and then we'll try and get off without being seen."

They left their compartment and there were people in the hall outside, trying to get through with their suitcases. They were going one way, while Clint and Sally tried to move against the traffic, drawing dirty looks from others.

" . . . supposed to disembark from the other end . . ." Clint heard someone say, but he ignored the comment and kept moving.

Once they were between cars he said to Sally, "Stay here, I want to take a look."

Clint moved to the edge and leaned forward so he could get a better look at the station than he was able to get from the train window; at the same time he tried not to lean too far out.

People had started to leave the train, and were being met by others. Among the groups who were hugging and shaking hands, Clint could see five or six men who were just loitering about, trying to look inconspicuous.

They're probably Cartwright's men, he thought, but he couldn't afford to take that chance.

"Come on," he said, taking hold of Sally's arm.

"Where?"

"We're going to get off on the other side of the train."

"But everyone's disembarking on this side," she said. "Wouldn't it be better if we try to blend in with the crowd?"

"There are at least six men out there who are expecting us to blend in with the crowd," he said. "They won't expect us to move away from the crowd."

"Are you sure about this?"

"Have I steered you wrong up to now?" he asked. She opened her mouth to answer and he grabbed her arm and said, "Never mind, just come on."

In the station Del Stark's sharp eyes were missing nothing—but so far there was nothing to miss. Sally Murcer had been described to him in detail by Robert Russell, so that he was not just going by the fact that she had red hair. He had enough information about her to pick her out even if she was disguised.

The simple fact of the matter was that she had not gotten off that train.

The next train from Chicago was not due in for seven hours, but Russell had assured him that Adams and the woman would be on this one.

Something was wrong.

William Cartwright was inside the station while his men were on the platform, where they could get a good look at the disembarking passengers. By the time Cartwright—inexperienced as a field man—decided that *he* should also be on the platform, where Clint Adams could recognize him, it was too late.

Clint and Sally found a door they could use to leave the train by the opposite side. He dropped to the ground first, since there was no platform, and then helped Sally down.

He had just caught her when someone shouted, "Hey, you can't get off on that side!"

Clint ignored the man and said to Sally, "Let's move."

"Hey," the man shouted even louder, "you can't do that. Hey you!"

"Come on," Clint said, pushing Sally ahead of him, "before some hears him."

Del Stark heard the man shouting and knew instinctively what was happening. He moved quickly to the train and leaped up onto it where two of the cars joined, climbed over the safety chains and made his way to the other side. He dropped down and looked around and just saw them as they turned a corner behind a building. A man and a woman.

It had to be them.

Clint and Sally moved away from the train they had come in on and began to weave between railroad cars in the Washington railroad yard. Abruptly, they stopped between cars while Clint got his bearings.

"Do you know where we're going?" she asked him.

"Don't worry," he said, "I'm a little more at home here in Washington than I was in either Denver or Chicago."

Sally watched his face as he looked around and decided that she didn't believe him. However, she also decided not to call him on it. Whatever he knew about Washington, it was plenty more than *she* did.

As she had been all along, she was in his hands and she simply had to trust his judgment.

Chapter Forty-Two

After they made their successful escape from the train station and the train yard, Clint actually found himself in a section of Washington he recognized. He hadn't wanted to worry Sally by telling her he didn't *really* know his way around, and now he didn't have to. He had been to this section of Washington one time in the past, and knew of a hotel not far away.

Sally started to feel better after they got away from the train yard. Clint *seemed* to know where he was going, and she found that—at least—comforting.

"How much farther?" she asked, just to test him.

"A few blocks," he said. "There's a hotel called the Les Roberts—at least, there was the last time I was here."

"Who was Les Roberts that they named a hotel after him?" she asked.

"I don't know," he said. "Probably some kind of minor politician. Anyway, there it is."

Sally looked up and saw a worn out two-story building with a faded sign out front that said: LES ROBERTS.

Now she *did* feel better.

Del Stark followed Clint Adams and Sally Murcer at a discreet distance. He knew he could have killed them right there in the street, but that would have made it necessary to shoot Clint Adams in the back. When Stark killed the Gunsmith, he wanted the man to see it coming—and he didn't want stories being told in the future about how he had shot the Gunsmith in the back.

He tracked them to a hotel called the Les Roberts, and watched them go inside.

Standing across the street he was wondering who the hell Les Roberts was that someone had named a hotel after him?

"One room," Clint told the desk clerk.

"Of course, sir," the clerk said with a knowing smile.

Sally wanted to tell the man it wasn't what he thought it was, but then she realized that—in part, at least—it was. The man obviously thought they were going to have sex in the room, and if Sally had her way, they were, so she decided there was really nothing to get insulted about.

On the way up to the room she realized that she felt insulted, anyway.

• • •

Once they were in the room Sally asked, "Now what?"

"Now you stay here while I figure out a way to get a message to the government."

"You want me to stay here alone?"

He walked to the window and looked out. The room overlooked an alley, so he couldn't see the street in front of the hotel. He didn't *think* they were followed, but he was better at following a trail than he was at picking someone up following *his*—especially in the city.

He turned and looked at Sally and said, "You've got the New Line. Keep it handy, and keep the door locked."

"When will you be back?"

"Just as soon as I get word to Cartwright," he said. "It shouldn't take me too long."

"I hope not," she said. "I'm anxious to get this over with."

"So am I," he said. He took her by the shoulders, kissed her briefly and said, "Be back soon."

"Be careful," she said. "Maybe I should come to back you up."

"Uh-uh, no, not this time," he said. "This time *you* listen to *me*. All right?"

She nodded and said, "All right."

He moved to the door, opened it, looked back and reminded her, "Lock it," and left, closing it behind him. He stood in the hall until he heard the lock click, and then went downstairs.

Del Stark debated whether he should go inside and ask the clerk for their room number, but decided against it. He figured Adams would probably come out pretty quickly once he got the girl settled. He had to get word to the government that the girl was alive.

He only had to wait a few minutes to see that he was right. Clint Adams came out of the front of the hotel, looked around, and then started off the way they had come. Stark had two choices. He could follow Clint Adams, pick a spot and confront him, or he could let him go and kill the girl. He was being paid, after all, to kill the *girl*. The Gunsmith was just a bonus, but he was a bonus Stark might lose if he let the man get away. Adams was sure to return with some help, and then Stark would have to take a big chance in order to kill him.

He decided to go after Adams first, and then come back for the girl.

He gave Clint a good head start, then stepped from his doorway and followed.

Cartwright was beside himself.

The train station had emptied out and there was still no sign of Adams or the girl. They had either missed the train, or they had gotten by him and his men. Cartwright *knew* that he wasn't a field man, so the chances that Adams had gotten by him were quite good.

"What do we do now, sir?" one of his men asked.

"Ask around," Cartwright said. "Someone might have seen them."

"The passengers are all gone, sir," the man said.

"Then talk to the railroad people," Cartwright said, patiently. "The conductor, people from the yard. Anyone. *Someone* must have seen them."

"If they were on the train," the man said.

Cartwright glared at the man and asked, "What's your name?"

"Gar Haywood, sir," the man said.

"Haywood, just do as I tell you and let *me* worry about the possibilities, okay?"

"Uh, yes, sir," the man said. "Right away, sir."

Haywood walked over to four men and one woman and relayed the orders he had received from Cartwright. Cartwright stared at the people, recognizing all but the woman. How many female operatives did he have, anyway? He couldn't remember—and why the hell was he wondering about that now?

"Damn," he muttered, "I'm getting senile."

He walked over to the six operatives and said, "What's the holdup, Haywood?"

"Uh, none, sir," the young operative said. "We're just getting underway now."

"Leave the young lady with me and take the others with you."

"Yes, sir."

"What's you name?" Cartwright asked the woman.

"Dawson, sir," she said, "Janet Dawson."

"Miss?"

"Yes, sir," she said. "I'm not married."

He wondered why. She was young, and attractive.

"All right," he said, "you and I are going to question whatever people are left in the station."

"Yes, sir," she said. "What am I looking for, sir?"

Jesus, he thought, what I wouldn't give for some experienced field operatives. Where were Jim West and Ross Martin when he needed them?

"Find me someone who saw Adams and the girl, Miss Dawson," he said. "Find *some*one."

"Yes, sir," she said. "I'll do that."

As she walked away he hoped she would, but somehow he doubted it.

William Masters Cartwright had to admit it. After years of being hard on his operatives, trying to get the best out of them, he himself had screwed up. If Adams and the girl had made it to Washington and ended up dead, it was going to be his fault for not giving them the proper coverage.

If Adams ended up dead, he was going to resign.

Chapter Forty-Three

Clint was wondering how to get a message to Cartwright short of walking right up to the man's office when he saw a boy of about twelve on the street in front of a saloon. The boy was begging for pennies, or offering shoeshines in return. Clint approached the boy, who saw him coming and figured him for a mark.

"How about it, mister?" the boy asked. "I got a sister and an invalid mother to support."

"Are you sure that's not a mother and an invalid sister?" Clint asked.

The boy frowned for a moment and then said, "No, I think I got it right—hey!"

"Forget it, son," Clint said. "How would you like to make a dollar?"

"Wow!" the boy said, then frowned suspiciously and asked, "Doing what?"

"Just delivering a message."

"To who?"

"A friend of mine."

"What kind of message?" the boy asked. "It better be short, I ain't got too good a memory."

"I'll write it down," Clint said. He dug out a paper and pencil and wrote a short note to Cartwright, telling the man to meet him on a street corner he knew was about three blocks from the hotel. As a matter of fact, it was *the* street corner he was on.

"Here," Clint said, handing the boy the note and fifty cents.

"Hey," the boy said, "this is only *half* a dollar."

"Do I look like I was born yesterday?" Clint asked the boy. "When you come back you'll get the other half."

The boy thought it over a moment, then said, "Okay."

"Get going."

"Mister . . ."

"What?"

"Did you know you was being followed?"

Clint had the urge to turn around and look, but quelled it.

"Are you sure?"

"I may have a bad memory," the boy said, "but I got great eyesight. There's a man following you. He's about a block back, but he's standing there watching us now."

Clint reached into his pocket and brought out four more bits and handed them to the boy.

"What's your name?" he asked as the boy accepted the money with a surprised look.

"Chris Rand."

"Well, Chris," Clint said, "what's the man look like?"

"He's tall, pretty old—"

"How old?"

"Old as you, probably."

Clint smiled to himself. To a twelve year old that was pretty old.

"What's he wearing?"

"A suit, dark, and a dark, flat-brimmed hat."

"Is he armed?"

"Can't see for sure from here, but if he's following you, what do you think?"

"You been inside this saloon?"

"I'm only twelve—"

"Cut it out," Clint said.

"Yeah, I been inside."

"It have a back door?"

"Nope," the kid said, "but it's got a side door right behind the bar."

"Fine," Clint said. "Take that message to the train station. If the man isn't there you'll have to go to his office. I've written the address on the paper."

"What does the man look like?"

"You'll know him," Clint said. "He'll look worried, *very* worried."

Clint hadn't seen Cartwright at the train station, but if Sally Murcer was as important to the government as she was supposed to be, it figured that the man would be there. If he'd been smart he would have stood where Clint could see him, but then Cartwright was used to working behind a desk, and not in the field.

"Okay. Get going and deliver that message. When you come back, I'll give you another dollar."

The boy put the money in his pocket and said, "Do me a favor."

"What?"

"Stay alive until I come back."

Clint said, "I'll do my best," and meant it.

Del Stark watched the byplay between Clint Adams and the boy and pieced together what was happening. Apparently Adams didn't want to directly approach his government contact, so he was sending a note with the boy. Well, that was fine. By the time anyone responded to the note, both Adams *and* the girl would be dead.

As Stark watched, the boy accepted the note and probably payment from Adams and ran off. Adams turned and went into the saloon. That was fine with Stark. That rundown saloon was as good a place as any for their meeting.

Their first and final meeting.

Chapter Forty-Four

Clint entered the saloon and approached the bar. There were three other men in the place, one sitting alone, and two sharing a table. All three looked like they had been sitting there since the place opened, drinking for the entire four or five hours.

"What'll you have?" the bored bartender asked.

"Put a beer on the bar," Clint said, "and I want to use your side door."

Clint knew the request was probably unusual, but the man reacted without any change of expression and said, "You gonna use the door before or after you pay for the beer?"

Del Stark took his time approaching the saloon. He wasn't in a hurry. It would take the boy time to get where he was going to deliver his message, and then it would take some time for the man or

172

men who responded to the message to make their way back. Stark wanted to savor this. He did most of his work here in the East, but he knew very well who the Gunsmith was, and what it would mean to him to be known as the man who had killed him.

He walked very slowly to the front of the saloon.

Sally decided she couldn't wait. She had only been alone in the hotel for a few minutes and already she was starting to go crazy. She tucked the New Line into her belt, underneath her shirt, and left the hotel room.

Chris Rand was a fast runner, and the man who had paid him a dollar had told him that if he was fast enough he'd be able to deliver the message at the train station. If not he was going to have to go to some office. Chris decided he would rather deliver it at the train station, which was much closer. In fact, the boy was sure that he had reached the train station even before the man had been able to find the side door to the saloon.

When Chris entered the station he saw a man and a woman standing together. The man was shaking his head, and the woman was talking. Chris knew he had the right man because this one looked *very* worried.

"Mister?" he said, approaching the man.

The man looked at him and said, "Not now, son."

"But mister—"

"I said not now!"

"Here, boy," the woman said, handing him a nickel. "Now go away."

Chris took the nickel and knew he was going to have to do something to get the man's attention.

"Mister!"

"Jesus, kid," the man said, "get lost. Can't you see I'm busy?"

Chris would have walked away, except he wanted that other dollar, so he did the only thing he could think of.

He kicked the man in the shin.

Clint went out the side door and worked his way down the alley to the front of the building. He peered around the front and saw a man approaching the saloon slowly. The man matched the description the boy had given him. The two dollars he was paying the boy was well worth it.

He waited there at the mouth of the alley until the man finally entered the saloon. He was in no hurry, which led Clint to believe that the man was a pro. He slipped from the alley and moved cautiously to the front of the saloon.

Del Stark entered the saloon and looked around. He saw one man sitting at a table alone, his head drooping; two men sitting together, both turning their heads to stare at him from behind bleary eyes; a bartender standing at the bar, holding a rag; and a full beer sitting on the bar.

He knew he'd been had.

Chapter Forty-Five

Sally ran down the street and thought she saw Clint standing in front of a rundown looking saloon. She started to call out to him, but thought better of it. Instead, she slowed to a walk and started for the saloon just as Clint entered.

Clint looked through the door of the saloon and saw the back of the man who had just entered. From the set of the man's shoulders he had just realized that he'd been outflanked.

Del Stark put his hand inside his jacket and came out with a .45 with a cutdown barrel. He heard the creak of floorboard behind him and knew that Adams was behind him.

• • •

"You want to stand fast," Clint said to the man. He took one step inside the doorway.

"That you, Adams?" the man asked.

"It's me," Clint said. "You want to tell me why you were following me?"

"You spotted me?" the man asked. "I must be slipping."

"I didn't spot you," Clint said, "the kid I was with did."

The man laughed, a dry laugh, and said, "I must *really* be slipping."

"I don't think so," Clint said. "The kid was pretty street smart. What's your name."

"Stark," the man said, "Del Stark. Mean anything to you?"

"No, should it?"

"Not really," Stark said. "I do most of my work in the East. I know you, though."

"I figured," Clint said. "You after me or the girl?"

"I'm being paid for the girl," Stark said.

"Seems to me you could have had her easy," Clint said.

"Could have," Stark said, "but I consider you a bonus."

"Went for the bonus first, huh?"

The man shrugged. Both of his hands were still out of sight, and Clint was pretty sure he was holding a gun in one of them.

"What do we do now?" Clint asked.

"This was a nice move," Stark said, inclining his head toward the beer on the bar. "How'd you know this place had another door?"

"I asked the kid."

"Jesus," Stark said, shaking his head, "mucked up by a kid."

"I repeat," Clint said, "what do we do now?"

"Don't know," Stark said. "What do you suggest?"

"You could drop your gun and walk out of here, and keep walking," Clint suggested.

"I think you know I can't do that," Stark said. "I'd have to stop working if I did that."

"I guess you would."

"You could let me turn around and get set," Stark said.

"Doing most of your work in the East," Clint said, "I don't imagine you do most of your killing that way."

"No, that's true," Stark said.

"That pretty much makes you a dead man," Clint said.

He looked over at the bartender, who did something odd then. He folded his arms in front of him, but with his right hand he simulated a gun. Was he telling Clint that Stark was holding a gun in his *right* hand?

"I'm going to turn around anyway, Adams," Stark said. "I'm left-handed, so I'm going to hold out my left hand. See? No gun."

Stark held out his empty left hand and started to turn.

"Bad idea, Stark!" Clint said.

"Only one I got, Adams," Stark said. "You forced this by outflanking me. My mistake, and one of us has got to pay for it."

Stark was turning to his left, his empty hand held away from him. He had turned almost completely and

Clint was ready for the sudden move as he swung his right hand into view.

Clint drew and fired and Stark grunted as the bullet struck him. The gun fell from his right hand but he stayed on his feet long enough to say, "Damn, you're as f-fast as they s-say . . ." and then he fell.

Clint walked over to the body, checked it, and made sure it was dead, then holstered his gun. He walked to the bar, picked up the beer and took a couple of swallows.

"Thanks for the tip," he said to the bartender.

The bartender held up his right hand, simulated a gun, and blew on his index finger/barrel.

Sally Murcer came running in, saw Clint at the bar and said, "Thank God."

"Draw the lady a beer," Clint said to the bartender.

The bartender nodded, and at that point the front door opened again and William Masters Cartwright burst in—that is, he *limped* in, for some reason—with a bunch of men behind him.

"There's a brat outside who says you owe him a dollar," Cartwright said.

"Beers for them, too?" the bartender asked.

"Sure," Clint said, "why not? The government's paying."

The bartender shook his head and said, "Business ain't been this good in months."

Robert Russell looked across his desk at Nelson Coleman.

"I only have one more chance," he said.

"What's that?" Coleman asked.

"You."

"What do you mean?" Coleman asked, and then, "You don't mean you want *me* to kill them?"

"It would be worth a lot to you," Russell said, "a lot more than you've been getting."

"For information," Coleman said, shaking his head, "*not* for killing. That's not my—I can't *do* that."

"If I get convicted," Russell said, "so does everyone who helped me. Think about that."

Stunned, Nelson Coleman left Russell's office. He was even more stunned when he was stopped and arrested right outside the building by Secret Service personnel. After his initial shock, however, he was actually *relieved*.

"I want to talk," he said to the men who had arrested him.

"Don't worry," one of them—Gar Haywood, actually—said, "you will."

Clint Adams and Sally Murcer were in a hotel room at the Washington House Hotel. It was a suite, being paid for by the government. Clint thought that Cartwright had given in pretty quickly about putting them both up in the same suite, but figured that the man was paying some private penance.

They were lying together in bed, now, having just made love.

"Tomorrow's the day," Sally said. "After that I'm on my own."

"And safe."

"Yes," she said, "and safe."

"Where will you go?" he asked.

"I figured I'd take the train back to Denver, and then figure it out from there. What about you?"

"That's quite a coincidence," he said. "I'll be going back to Denver myself, to pick up Duke."

"We could travel together," she said.

"Yes," he said, "we could—and this time we could actually enjoy it."

ANGEL EYES *series*
by
Award-Winning Author
Robert J. Randisi (J.R. Roberts)

Visit us at www.speakingvolumes.us

TRACKER *series*
by
Award-Winning Author
Robert J. Randisi (J.R. Roberts)

Visit us at <u>www.speakingvolumes.us</u>

MOUNTAIN JACK PIKE *series*
by
Award-Winning Author
Robert J. Randisi (J.R. Roberts)

Visit us at www.speakingvolumes.us

Sign up for free and bargain books

Join the Speaking Volumes mailing list

Text

ILOVEBOOKS

to 22828 to get started.